"You're in no shape to travel."

Rosalind's fingers curled. She had more sense than to translate Armel's words into sympathy. Whatever his reason for wanting to keep her there, it was certainly not that.

"There's always your aunt," Rosalind said on a note of desperation. "She's a woman. She would listen."

"No doubt she would, being notoriously kindhearted. But rest assured, whatever her personal opinion, she would not go against me." Armel shook his head dryly, as if both her threats and herself were without substance.

"No, Rosalind. You will rest for a while as I seek to uncover any further deception. Then, when I have you straightened out, we will decide sensibly what is to become of you."

OTHER

Harlequin Romances

by MARGARET PARGETER

The Jewelled Caftan

by

MARGARET PARGETER

Harlequin Books

TORONTO · LONDON · NEW YORK · AMSTERDAM
SYDNEY · HAMBURG · PARIS

Original hardcover edition published in 1978
by Mills & Boon Limited

ISBN 0-373-02211-5

Harlequin edition published November 1978

CHAPTER ONE

Ross, short for Rosalind, Lindsay, lay on her side on the harsh, sandy floor of a tent in the heart of the desert. At least, she supposed drearily, it must be somewhere pretty isolated, miles from civilisation—some unknown outpost on the wild Moroccan border? The floor of the tent seemed to be swarming with legions of lice which crawled feather-like over her sensitive skin, their bites setting up a burning irritation. With only one hand it was impossible to ward them off!

Both her ankles were bound to a hastily driven stake with a thin piece of rope, her left arm being tied securely behind her back in much the same way. Her captors had left her right hand free only that she might stop the infiltrating dust from choking her. The longer she lay the more fervently did she wish they had not done so, as the thought of death was beginning to seem quite pleasant compared to the discomfort of this!

Since noon yesterday and all through the night she had lain here. Now the sun was high again, so they must be well into another day. Feverishly she wondered how much longer she was expected to bear it? Her head ached so badly she was having some difficulty in focusing, and the last few drops of water she had been given had done nothing but add to the torture she had already endured.

Outside, at this hour of day, there would be no sun, just the glare of white-hot sky that shrivelled the eyes and skin, burning everything it touched. Not that this appeared to affect the desert men, the dark-skinned nomads who held Ross and her companions. Hazily she pondered which barbaric tribe they might belong to. From here she could hear their shouts of wild laughter, the incomprehensible curses which chilled the blood—if anything could in this unbelievable oven! On a gasp of helpless, half hysterical protest Ross twisted and turned until again she collapsed, exhausted. She tried unsuccessfully, for what seemed to be almost the hundredth time to escape the cruel thongs which held her, knowing, for about the first time in her short life, what true fear really was.

Eventually her mind blacked out—not in sleep, for she could still dimly hear the noise around the tent, but in a kind of merciful oblivion. Vaguely she became aware that the three boys who had been travelling with her and who were likewise tied had begun whispering to each other. It was as if something had alerted them, but as she happened to be on the opposite side of the large tent she was unable to make out what they were saying. Nor could she arouse herself sufficiently to ask. Their voices were necessarily low as they had soon, and painfully, discovered that their captors did not like them talking even among themselves!

Whatever it was about, the mumble went on, but when one of the older men hissed her name it only fell on deaf ears. Ross, floating temporarily in the arms of a peculiar delirium, felt like a sleepwalker, in no great hurry to return from the beguilingly cool depth of her imagination.

She was home again in England, at Springfield, a place she had never cared for greatly but which now seemed the most desirable place on earth. What a perfect fool she had been to leave it! How the relative she had lived with and worked for would laugh if she could see her now. No, that might not be strictly true! Cynthia might be worried out of her head if she knew of her predicament, which was one good reason to be thankful she did not! She might not be surprised, though, as hadn't she always considered Ross too impulsive for her own good? She imagined Ross was spending three quiet weeks in Cornwall with Freddy's cousin Avis!

A low moan of despair escaped Ross's half-conscious lips. If only she had known what she was letting herself in for! Yet didn't other people do much the same sort of thing without anything going wrong? Part of her mistake, she realised, lay in choosing the wrong company. If she had consulted one of the many reliable travel agents and gone for a properly organised tour, how much wiser she might have been today!

Painfully her mind wandered, crazed more than a little by thirst. Trying to hold on to her last dregs of sanity, she forced her thoughts back to Springfield, the large, shabby old house on the edge of the sprawling industrial town where she had lived with Cynthia for the past two years. Freddy, too, when he had been at home.

Why did she have to think of it in the past tense when it would still be there? Suppressing another moan, she thought of it as it would be around this time of day, brooding and quiet, waiting for Cynthia coming home for lunch. If Ross hadn't been so discontented with her lot she might have been there with her, although she was generally forced through pressure of work to make do with a sandwich in the office. Cynthia would never hear of her having a holiday abroad— and perhaps she had been proved right. Ross had wanted to travel, see something of the world, but she could see now that this was no excuse for the sheer irresponsibility of her behaviour! She was young, it wouldn't have done her any harm to have waited a little longer.

Stirring again, Ross sighed deeply, her slender body tormented by heat. It was her father who had been indirectly responsible for this urge to travel, having, years ago, filled her childish ears with stories of his adventures. He had been a foreign correspondent and, when he was still alive, she had used to hang breathlessly on to his every word. His trips around the world, the people he had met, the tight corners he had been in. She could still remember.

He had talked a lot about the Middle East, especially of the desert. This seemed always to have been his great love. She could recall his saying as if it had been yesterday: 'The Sahara is a big place, my darlings, the largest desert in the world. It's so vast a man could lose himself and never be seen again.' It had mostly been for Freddy's benefit, of course, as he was older, but Ross had been the more absorbed.

Occasionally he had taken their mother there on holiday, but always left Ross and Freddy with Cynthia, who appeared to be the only relative they had. Freddy was Ross's half-brother, her mother having already been married once before she had met John Lindsay. Freddy was the child of her first marriage.

Then there had been that terrible time when their parents had both been killed returning from Morocco. She and Freddy had been sent to an orphanage—in care, Cynthia had preferred to put it. She couldn't take them personally as she had a large business to run, but she had kept a distant eye on them. Freddy, because of his age, had only been there a short while but Ross had spent years there. Afterwards she had trained as a secretary and worked for Cynthia ever since.

Ross didn't particularly like this relative who was so distantly removed as to scarcely be a relative at all, but she knew she should be grateful for what Cynthia had done for them, and she did try to do her best. As well as the office she helped in the house, which she didn't really care for either as it was so big and old and cold, but the fields outside were another thing. At weekends, when Cynthia often lunched and dined with friends and clients, Ross spent hours in the fields and cool summer woods with her sketch pad. At this she excelled—not that she got much encouragement. Cynthia was always telling her there was no future in it. Not her kind of art, anyway.

The trouble was, Cynthia never did see talent of any sort in Ross at all, although she had proved more than satisfactory in the office. It never ceased to puzzle Ross that Cynthia was much more tolerant of Freddy, who never seemed to succeed at anything and certainly never put himself out to please her. He had been a bright but lazy teenager and Cynthia had paid out of her own pocket for him to go to a good school. Here he had done very little, but even when he had been sent down from university, she had still made excuses for him. Now he spent most of his time in London, only coming home when he was broke. Often for months Ross never saw him, yet she could never forget he was her half-brother.

The wind, or sirocco, as it was called in Morocco, whined hotly around the tent. Numbly Ross tried to lick her cracked lips with a partly swollen tongue, but was aware of no relief, only pain. Inside the anorak she was wearing sweat ran in rivulets down her tender skin, soaking the cotton in dark patches, but she dared not unzip it as the nomads had not yet discovered she was a girl. When they were first captured Freddy had assured her hastily that it was much safer that they should think of her as an impracticably slender boy.

One thing puzzled her greatly. While Freddy and the other two men, although bound as she was, had been given moderate amounts of food and water, she had been offered nothing. If it hadn't been for the young serving lad who had furtively wetted her mouth, as if feeling sorry for her, she doubted if she could have survived.

Her mind, as if wholly concentrated on water, wandered tenaciously back to Springfield, to a small deep well she had found one day in the woods, fed by a clear, crystal spring. What wouldn't she give for just one cupful of it! Water was something she had never actively appreciated before, along with other things. Ruefully she wondered why she had ever wanted to leave Cynthia, why she had ever listened to Freddy.

It was he who had persuaded Ross to join this supposedly exciting trip across North Africa. He had seemed so flatteringly keen to have her company. She had not known then that he was financially bereft again.

Ross was due for a holiday, she hadn't in fact had one since she had started work. 'If you cash the few hundred Dad left you,' Freddy had urged, 'we could be there and back within three weeks.'

Freddy had already explained that two of his friends were leaving by truck from London, but to make it an economical proposition they needed two more. If Ross would oblige them by coming as cook it would solve a lot of problems. She and Freddy could fly out and join them, which would cut down considerably on the time they need be away.

'Leave everything to me,' he had told her, when eventually he talked her into agreeing. 'I'll deal with old Cynthia!'

From then on Freddy had taken over. He hit on the bright idea of telling Cynthia that they would tour, probably stay-

ing in Cornwall where, on his father's side, he did have a
cousin. Ross had never met this cousin, nor had Cynthia, but
Freddy said she was a lot like him.

'I'll see to it, and she can be relied on to send the odd
postcard, just to keep Cynthia happy,' he had said, craftily
eyeing Ross's doubtful face. 'Otherwise, old girl, you're
going to get nowhere.'

'I just don't care for the idea of deceiving anyone, least of
all Cynthia,' Ross had replied dubiously.

Freddy's discontented face had twisted. 'You don't deceive
someone who works you to death for a pittance,' he retorted
sarcastically, 'and who has scarcely a kind word to say to
you—or of you,' he had added frankly.

It was only too true! Unhappily, Ross had realised. Cynthia did seem to enjoy treating her like a kind of inferior
servant, forever telling her she was a nuisance and a liability
and that one day, if Ross worked hard, she might just
manage to get out of her debt. Ross wasn't altogether without spirit and often felt she could easily have left. Sometimes
she thought she stayed only because Cynthia seemed to be
getting old and she had done so much for Freddy. And,
after years in an orphanage, a home was a home, whatever
else it might be lacking.

'You really think I should, then?' Ross had still hesitated,
until the last moment, in spite of Cynthia's harshness, curiously reluctant to defy her, to enter such a complication of
conspiracy even for something she had always longed to do.

'Of course!' Seeing Ross weaken visibly, Freddy had
hastened to assure her that what they contemplated was
neither wicked or hurtful. 'I doubt if Cynthia will so much
as ask if you've enjoyed yourself, when you come back,' he
had said cynically, 'so I shouldn't worry about that. Don't
think about it any more,' he'd advised. 'Just go. Otherwise
you'll get cold feet and might never get another opportunity.'

So Ross, against her better judgment, had allowed herself
to be persuaded. Having drawn her only few hundred
pounds from the bank, she handed it over to Freddy, who
promised to use it with care. If it hadn't been accomplished

all too quickly she doubted if her nerve would have held. To be involved with Freddy, she soon discovered, was like going downhill on a huge roller—once started it seemed impossible to stop! Not that she had ever been able to decide if she really wanted to stop. In her head had raged a perpetual tug-of-war, but after Freddy had completed all the necessary arrangements she didn't see how she could back out, even had she wanted to.

Before she quite realised they were off in Freddy's old Mini, bound ostensibly for Cornwall, in reality Gatwick. From there they would fly to Casablanca. Cynthia had been too busy grumbling to ask many questions. She was only about sixty and her tongue had not yet lost its sharpness. She had agreed waspishly to allow Ross a short holiday, but warned her that if she wasn't back on time she need not bother to come at all. Also she had refused to pay her for the time she would be away and, although it would only have been a few pounds, Ross had been counting on it. Having to do without it had meant not being able to buy any new clothes, as Freddy had taken almost all her savings. However, he had convinced her she would only need a pair or two of old jeans and that they couldn't take much on the plane anyway.

The flight itself had not been momentous. Ross, keyed up with a rising excitement which had melted away the last of her regrets, had been surprised to find how quickly it had passed. With Freddy by her side, comfortingly familiar, she had felt completely safe. Too soon they were landing at the airport at Casablanca and she caught her first sight and sound of the mysterious East which she had wanted to visit for so long.

Ross knew, despite everything, that she would never forget her first glimpse of it. Even as they left the plane the impact of a thousand tantalising impressions hit her, an inexplicable assault on already quivering emotions. For a long moment she had stood hesitantly, not knowing how best to cope with such an intensity of feeling. There had been within her some indescribable desire to respond to some pagan-like element in the air around her, and yet another agonising impression that the gods were already laughing at her because, in her innocence, she didn't know how!

Freddy had stared frowning at her suddenly rapt face and made a sharply trite remark to break the spell. 'Come on, small sister,' he had said. 'You don't have to stand here like some moonstruck gazelle! Come and meet the boys. I want them to imagine you're practical, not a dreamer. They wouldn't thank me for one of those.'

It was then that Ross had known her first shock of unease. Freddy's friends, Lance and Denis, hadn't been at all as she had pictured them. Freddy, although they didn't really have a lot in common, was family, and fair, like herself. They both shared their mother's pale gold colouring which made them look much younger than they actually were. Freddy, of course, was much taller and heavier, but he did have an engagingly innocent appearance, if, in his case, it was oddly deceptive. One only had to look a little closer at Freddy to see that, at twenty-six, lines of dissipation were already forming on his attractive face.

Ross didn't notice. If she had done so she did not have the experience to judge the degree of such things. All she knew was what she felt instinctively about his friends. Even then it was merely a kind of dawning apprehension, not anything she might have put into words. They didn't appear to take a great deal of notice of her at first, but she soon became conscious of their too intimate glances, their low-voiced suggestive remarks, all of which seemed to confirm her first doubtful reactions.

When, on the second day, she had complained with some embarrassment to Freddy, he had told the erring pair quite frankly to knock it off. 'Though you can't blame them too much, Ross,' he pointed out later. 'I guess I tend to forget you're growing up!'

Lance and Denis, like him, were in their middle twenties, and, to Ross's dismay, she quickly realised they belonged to entirely different worlds. Their crudeness and cynicism amazed and startled her. They might have been years older than they actually were! Overhearing a lot of conversation which was probably not meant for her ears, she got the impression there was not one place they hadn't exploited in their drifting, idle lives. Not one experience they hadn't sampled. If it occurred to Ross that Freddy was greatly at fault by bringing her anywhere near such men she could see, at this stage, there was little to be gained by airing such views. In spite of his half-hearted protests, they didn't stop to spare her blushes, seeming to derive a great delight from the often shocked expressions that chased across Ross's vividly expressive young face.

'How did you ever come to know them?' she had asked in a fierce aside to Freddy one evening after supper, which she had cooked to a battery of blatant remarks. 'I think they're positively beastly, and you must have known I'd never have come if I'd realised that they were like this. I don't know how you ever came to have such friends!' she had choked.

'Oh, come off it, Ross!' Too aware of his niggling conscience, he sounded frankly fed up. 'They aren't all that bad. It's just their manner, which I admit occasionally leaves a bit to be desired. But you can't go round with your head in the sand much longer, if you'll forgive the pun, seeing how we're sitting on tons of the stuff. Isn't it about time you grew up?'

'It's more than overdue, I would say!' Lance, having caught Freddy's last few words, leered suggestively, and the way in which his eyes had gone over her thin but well curved figure had brought a hot blush to Ross's pale cheeks.

'Well, you haven't come to any harm yet, have you!' Freddy had intervened swiftly, before Ross could reply. He was pouring what she supposed was meant to be oil on troubled waters, but she suspected with sudden and frightening intuition that he was secretly rather nervous of his friends himself!

After that Ross had hated the lot of them, and if Freddy had not held all her money she would not have stayed. He had refused to even give her her return ticket, so there was little else she could do but tag along. He must have said something to the other two about her threatening to leave as, after that, they had been a little more restrained, but it wasn't anything for which Ross felt particularly grateful.

Taking precautions which she had never thought she would
be forced to resort to, she took to wearing as much concealing clothing as she could find. Her hair, too, with little
appreciation of its rare loveliness, she pinned tightly on top
of her head, jamming it securely beneath her wide-brimmed
hat which she didn't remove until she slept at night. She did
all this so that she might pass unnoticed. It was not until
they had been in the desert for almost three days that she
discovered it was not her all-enveloping anorak that was
distracting the attention of the two men. It was gold!

After Denis and Lance met them at the airport they had
gone immediately into Casablanca, and when Denis and
Lance had left to conclude some mysterious business Freddy
had shown her briefly around. He had been here before,
although Ross hadn't been aware of it until that moment,
when he declared idly that he must have forgotten to mention it. Ross had stared at him, curiously uneasy, while
knowing subconsciously that to reproach him would merely
be a waste of time. As if to make up for such an omission he
had made himself extremely pleasant, but somehow Ross had
not been able to put it from her mind. She had wandered
with him down palm-lined boulevards, through sun-kissed
parks and narrow twisting streets, noting also the many fine
examples of modern planning, but somehow the brightness
of the day had diminished.

Ross had not really thought about how they would spend
the next few days. If she had considered at all she had merely
concluded that they would probably make for Rabat, then up
the coast to Tangier, going slowly but trying to cover as
much ground as sensibly possible in three weeks. When
Freddy told her they were moving straight into the desert,
she felt puzzled but not unduly alarmed.

They travelled in a rough truck and the canvas-covered
back seemed to get unbearably hot. It was a hundred and
fifty miles to Marrakesh where the men obtained necessary
equipment and permits, and many more after that before
they came to Zagora and the Draa valley.

They camped beside the Mhamid oasis on the second
night. It was flat desert country with the occasional clump of

mountains outlined against the sky. Next morning they packed their gear and followed a track across a waste of pebbles and rock which eventually gave way to sandy desert. They were gone, almost before daylight, and it was only then that Ross had learnt about the gold.

Lost in the fascinating wonder of a pearly desert dawn, Ross eventually realised they had come to the end of the hard track and were travelling in what appeared to be a straight line over the Sahara. Undulating dunes stretched on either side, in what seemed a limitless, ruthless, sand-strewn wilderness. It might be exciting, but with a start she had questioned their wisdom in leaving the road.

Freddy, who had been sitting in the back of the truck beside her, had whispered, 'Shush! They've been here before, plenty of times. We're quite safe. They both know all the ropes. So do I, for that matter, and I don't want you to start making another fuss!'

'How do you mean?' She followed up her indignant gasp with a glance of pointed resentment.

Freddy's lips had tightened, and he had replied with exaggerated patience as he had stretched his cramped limbs in the confined space, 'Just that—that we're quite safe! You'll see as much of the primitive desert as you've been wanting to. We might even allow you to be there when we find the gold. Lance has all the maps.'

Incredulously Ross had stared at him. It was unbelievable, of course, the story they had about the Germans hiding gold in the Western Desert during the last war, and it never having been found. She might have laughed if she hadn't suddenly realised they were deadly serious. Even so, she found it difficult to credit that if gold had really been hidden, they imagined they had any chance of ever discovering exactly where it was.

Later, after a day of almost non-stop driving, she had asked Freddy if he didn't think they were quite crazy. She hadn't dared suggest this to Lance as already she was learning to be wary of him and wished to become the victim of his sarcastic remarks no more than was necessary. Freddy, while not annoyed because she was anxious, brushed her bewildered protests to one side.

'We've done a lot of research into this, Ross. We know what we're doing. We have, in fact, quite a bit of capital invested in it, so no one's going to stop us. Certainly not you, little sister!'

'But I never asked to be involved!' she had exclaimed. 'I wonder they wanted to bring a girl?'

'They didn't,' Freddy's shoulders had lifted in a careless shrug, 'but your money was the only way I could reach them. Why do you think I laid on the pressure, spent so many hours talking you into it? Don't tell me you'd be here if I'd left you to decide for yourself? I have you summed up all the way, Ross. Beneath that so cool exterior is an impulsive, high-spirited girl waiting to escape, but you did need that extra push.'

Ross felt ashamed, the way he put it. How could she deny that there was a lot of truth in what he said? She had allowed herself to be persuaded. That her recklessness might prove her eventual undoing was something she would rather not think about. Freddy must be right about the streak of wildness, otherwise she would not be here!

Subdued by a depressing weight of self-condemnation, she had suffered in silence for almost a week. For days, far away from the popular tourist routes, they had pressed on across the desert. Ross began to suffer badly. Instead of the pleasurable journey she had envisaged, spending a little time in towns and villages, she saw nothing but sand. This she wouldn't have minded in moderate doses, but she got no real satisfaction from interminable miles of it on ever hotter, sunscorched days! Very soon there had been very little water, scarcely enough to wash their hands, and at least one oasis on Lance's map, when they reached it, had dried out.

Ross's fine, pale skin, exposed too suddenly to long periods of sun, became burnt. Only her hat saved her creamy complexion, but even this was turning faintly brown. Sometimes she felt the truck resembled an oven. She was not allowed to sit in the front and no air seemed to penetrate the back, the vents all being closed to keep out the infiltrating sand. It was only a small truck, and, loaded with their gear and spare petrol, the space was cramped. The heat, especially around noon, could become so bad that Ross, crouched among all the paraphernalia, often felt almost unable to breathe. Often she would have given anything to have seen the last of it, but, contrarily, when it did break down she shared her companions' dismay.

'Oh, hell!' Lance had moaned with annoyance, as he surveyed the immobile vehicle. His eyes had swung angrily to the other two men. 'Can't either of you useless bastards do anything? Freddy, you're supposed to be the expert. One of the reasons you're here!'

Ross had bit back a splutter of surprise. Freddy, she could have told Lance, was expert at nothing, but the coarseness of his language warned her what to expect if he really lost his temper. She was probably better than Freddy when it came to engines. She didn't know a lot, but many a time she had fixed a small fault at home. The thought of home had made the sick feeling in her stomach worse and she had turned away.

A moment later she had been startled to hear Freddy mumble, 'I've never professed to be infallible, old boy. Ross here is almost as good as me. Between the two of us we'll see what we can do.'

That was how, Ross recalled painfully, she had been in such a mess when the desert men had arrived. Burst upon them would have been a better way of putting it! Grease from the engine had been plastered over her face and hands, even her hair had been smeared with a liberal coating of oil. After an hour they still hadn't found the fault, the whole of the engine being too covered in sand to make diagnosis easy. A lot of small, simple tests had been almost impossible to carry out with any degree of accuracy.

Time passed and Lance, heedless of Freddy's warning glances in Ross's direction, had got down to cursing long and loud. Ross, for once losing her own temper, had turned on him in a small fury and given him a piece of her mind. Lance, while his eyes had glinted with sudden interest, had merely raised his voice higher. Such had been the commotion

that they had never heard the nomads until they were within
a few yards of the truck.

Where they had come from Ross had no idea. One moment she could have sworn there was nothing, not even a
spot on the horizon, just miles of unmarked sand. The next,
they were surrounded, and Freddy had gasped hoarsely.

'Ross! For God's sake cover yourself up! Zip your jacket!
Don't let them see you're a girl until we know who they are.
They might be all right, but they don't look it to me!'

She had done her best—slid under the bonnet while she
had zipped up her anorak and jammed down her hat. She
supposed Freddy meant they could be gangsters. She had
never seen anything like them before, with their dark thin
faces and cruel slits of eyes. Before they had reached the
desert, in the few towns and villages they had passed
through, the people had been friendly and kind, not pushing, but polite and courteous, very willing, when asked, to
give helpful advice, and treating them in much the same way
as tourists were usually treated in England.

These men were different, she could see at a glance. They
might be, but they didn't look like the native Berbers. Not
that she knew if they were in Morocco any more, and the
Sahara was strewn with nomadic tribes who lived by their
own creeds, answerable only to themselves. For what had
seemed an incredible time the men had sat silently on their
thin, bony horses, just staring at them. Yet Ross had a
feeling they had been following the truck for a long while
and were not really surprised. Lance spoke to them in the
native Arabic which he knew very well, then in French.
Whether they understood or not there was no means of telling, as they had simply ignored his tentative efforts, breaking out into a gibberish language all of their own.

The truck had appeared to interest them greatly from the
start. A few of them, getting down from their horses, had
begun poking about it. Imagining it was because they had
never seen such a thing before, Ross was amazed when one
jumped into the driving seat and switched on the ignition.
His toothless leer of anticipation had swiftly turned to fury
when the engine refused to start and, although Lance tried

to explain, a rumble of anger swiftly swept through the gathering crowd of his friends. Several more of them left their mounts to grab hold of Ross and the three boys, shaking them roughly as they pointed with unmistakable meaning to the man at the wheel, but all Lance could continue to do was shake his head and, in turn, point to the tools they had been using trying to repair the engine.

Ross had felt faint. The grasp on her arms had been cruel and the hot reek from the men wrapped in their coarse burnouses had been terrible. Mindful of Freddy's warning, she had not dared struggle, but she had longed desperately to be free.

A young lad, whom she hadn't previously noticed, was eventually summoned from the crowd and a man who was obviously the leader spoke to him sharply. In halting French that surprised them the lad had managed to convey that they wanted the truck—and that it must be made to go!

This had brought a fresh sally of oaths from Lance. To Ross's horror the men had immediately bound his wrists and ankles and thrust a rough gag across his mouth before flinging him carelessly on to the sand. Another time Ross might have been glad that something had succeeded in shutting him up, but now she could only stare in terror, wondering what was to happen next.

The answer came quicker than she had anticipated, when the lad spoke again.

'My master says he will tie you all up, if you not mend truck.'

From then the whole affair seemed to turn into a fantastic nightmare. Feverishly Freddy and she had worked on the engine without success, while the sun had blazed down on their helpless heads. The man who drove could not fix an engine, the lad said. Ross gathered the truck would be a mark of some prestige with this wandering tribe and they were determined to have it. When it became apparent that neither Ross or Freddy could do anything the fury of the leader had been alarming. Immediately, in spite of Freddy's delaying tactics, they had been seized and bound like Lance and thrown down beside him.

To struggle against such numbers would have been futile, but as the men caught hold of Ross, to give Freddy his due, he had attacked them wildly with a spanner, catching the leader a glancing blow over his low brow and drawing blood.

'That's torn it!' Denis had exclaimed bitterly, as pandemonium had broken loose.

The naked venom in the eyes of the injured man had been frightening. Ross thought he must intend leaving them lying on the sand, tasty morsels for some roaming wild animal to pick up, but after scorching hours without food or attention a large black tent had been erected and all four dragged inside. Here some respite from the blazing sun had been more than offset by the way in which they had been tied firmly to hastily driven in posts—probably as an extra precaution until it was decided what to do with them, Lance had moaned.

Ross had been tied at one side of the tent, the boys on the other, but while they had at last been given something to eat and drink she had received nothing. If it hadn't been for the young lad who, as if feeling sorry for her, had furtively wetted her lips, she wasn't sure what she would have done. It puzzled her why she should be treated differently. When she had asked Lance, who happened to be nearest, his reply had been far from reassuring.

'They don't know you're a girl and probably think you're too small to be of much use.'

'Much use for what?'

'I'm not sure yet,' he had drawled laconically, 'but whatever they have in mind for us, don't worry. I've been in worse corners than this. It usually only takes a little patience.'

'And me?'

'Oh, they're possibly hoping you'll die of natural causes,' he had shrugged indifferently, regardless of Freddy's annihilating glance. 'Anything as fragile as you probably scares them stiff. However, if they knew you were a girl you might get better treatment!'

'Or then it could be worse!' Denis had laughed suggestively. 'Depends how you look at it.'

Now, a day later, by great effort, Ross aroused herself, pushing aside the too insidious thoughts of home. Whatever was going on outside, she couldn't even guess, but some instinct persuaded her to sit up and take notice. As if unconsciously to satisfy her curiosity, their young attendant crept in, informing them with innocent pleasure that someone had arrived and was fixing the engine, and that soon his master would be able to drive away. There was just one small matter to be decided first.

Ross longed to ask what this small matter was, but when she opened her mouth to speak no sound came. All she could manage was a hoarse, unintelligible croak which drew a frown of rather ashamed despair from Freddy.

Even had she managed to say anything there would have been no time for an answer, as almost immediately the flap of the tent burst open and two men came in. The boy was thrust rudely outside. The first man to enter was the leader. He was followed by another, a man so tall he was unable to stand upright but was forced to bow his head beneath the burning canvas. Ross didn't recall seeing him before. She was sure he had not been among the crowd who had watched her abortive attempt to get the truck going yesterday. He seemed a much larger type altogether than the small, wiry desert men.

Painfully, Ross screwed up her smarting eyes, staring at him blindly as he towered above her. Through a haze she saw that his face was dark, if not so dark as his companions, and the burnous he wore, though all-enveloping, was white. He appeared to have a kind of visible strength about him, and he looked clean. Clean . . . ! Lying, as she was, in so much dust and dirt, Ross doubted if she would ever be clean again!

She became aware that the nomad was making vigorous, enthusiastic gestures towards her with his hands, while his voice rose excitedly in a tongue she did not understand. He went so far as to poke her fiercely with his foot, as if she was a piece of merchandise he was trying hard to sell. As the thought struck her incongruously she blinked. If he was, then she knew suddenly that she would rather go with the tall man than be left here at the mercy of this other.

But apparently the tall one had no use for her either. After silently contemplating her slender, dirt-ingrained figure he turned contemptuously away. Despair caught Ross forcibly by the throat as she was forced to acknowledge his cold rejection. He was unimpressed by the boys too, as he spared them no more than an uninterested shrug. Clearly, whatever the purpose of his visit, it wasn't to rescue them.

Somehow Ross felt urgently that it was up to her to save them all, and she could only do this by acting now. But how? She couldn't speak to tell this newcomer she was a girl, which might have appealed to his sense of chivalry. Staring desperately at his broad back, she remembered reading somewhere—'If you can't escape your prison, try to change it for another that might offer better opportunities.'

There seemed sense in this, even to her slightly hysterical mind. Numbly she groped with strangely cold fingers for the zip of her anorak, rasping it down, exposing the unmistakable curves of her softly feminine body, tightly stretched against the thin, clinging material of her tee shirt.

As the tall stranger paused briefly in the doorway, the intensity of her gaze must have prompted him to turn his dark head. As he did so his eyes went straight to her, narrowing and glittering slightly with incredulous surprise. Then, as if bereft of words, he followed the nomad leader swiftly from the tent.

CHAPTER TWO

As soon as the flap of the tent dropped behind their formidable visitor Ross slumped, only managing to zip up her
anorak again before falling back to the ground. It had been
of no avail, her silly ruse hadn't worked. There had been no
sympathy on the man's face, merely contempt. If he was a
true Arab, of course, he would not appreciate immodesty in
a woman. Her small indiscretion, though prompted by desperation, had obviously only enraged him.

Her heart sank with a hopeless despair as she tried to raise
her head to look at the boys. The man had no intention of
having anything to do with any of them. He hadn't so much
as spared one kind word. When Freddy and Lance had
attempted to speak to him he had made no reply, and Ross
suspected it was not because he had not understood Freddy's
almost perfect French. Even Lance's fluent Arabic had
done nothing to merit an answer. He had no inclination to
do anything to help them out of their unfortunate position.
That, she decided, with a small quiver of rage, was how he
would consider it! The indifferent shrug of his broad shoulders as he had left had more than emphasised his unshake-
able Eastern philosophy.

'What Allah wills,' she guessed he would be saying to
himself. Not that Ross could believe God had much to do
with the predicament she was in now. It had been her own
fault, and all her humiliating attempts to put things right
had failed. In unforeseen ways she might inadvertently have
made their situation worse.

Slow, painful tears forced a desolate path down her sand-
hazed cheeks, but the peculiar lethargy was returning, anaes-
thetising to some extent her agony of mind. This time when
Ross's eyes closed she did not dream of home, the heat and
dust triumphing even over her imagination. The noisy splutter of an engine bursting into life a little later did not

register. Nor did the startled, low-voiced comments of the boys.

When the flap of the tent opened once again and Ross found herself roughly released from her bonds, she even felt a faint resentment at being disturbed. It was only after the ropes actually fell away that the subsequent pain in her limbs caused her to cry out, and, as if protesting against the returning circulation, she tried to fight the hands which set her free. The feeble endeavours of her protesting arms were instantly stilled with a quick word of command from a hard, decisive voice she had not expected to hear again. Instantly she felt herself grasped and lifted, taken outside and flung swiftly, with uncaring hands, across the front of a horse.

The impact of the saddle hurt, adding to the sharp soreness that seemed to be attacking every part of her body. Vaguely terrified, she thought of Freddy, still imprisoned in the horrible tent, but when she opened her eyes she saw beneath her only the wavering sand, and when she tried to speak, to beg whoever it was she was with to save him, her throat burned as before and no words came.

Ross was conscious of a man's arm holding her with all the restriction of an iron band, and that her face, hanging downwards, was pressed against a heavily muscled thigh. The tall man—if it was he who held her—was murmuring coldly, apparently to the nomads. '*Beslama*,' she heard him say, which she had learnt from Lance meant goodbye, and the thanks of the nomad leader, also in Arabic, followed them effusively as they rode away. The rogue sounded as if he was congratulating himself jubilantly, Ross decided bitterly. Hadn't he got the truck started and rid himself of a useless prisoner all on the same day?

Because of her unnatural position, slung like a sack over the horse, the ground danced crazily, and where only a few minutes ago she had longed to escape, now the crude tent she had left began, in retrospect, to take on all the advantages of a haven! Inevitably, in spite of the absorption with her thoughts, she began to feel sick. This turned the discomfort of her position into the kind of ordeal she had never known existed. Yet, when her weak struggles must have given some indication as to the degree of her suffering, the man's arm merely tightened, the depth of his antipathy mingling fiendishly with the cruel heat. The sand off the pounding hooves flew up in her face with a suffocating force so she could scarcely breathe, and she wondered how much longer she could stand it.

As they galloped the sound of the truck's engine faded in the distance and then there was nothing but silence broken by the dull thud of the horse. When at last it reared, the man bringing it to a sudden halt, Ross found herself lifted up and everything faded abruptly. With a small sigh she knew no more.

When she recovered consciousness she was not immediately aware of her surroundings. Stirring restlessly, she opened her eyes with a feeling she had slept for a very long time, the dreamless, heavy sleep that comes from sheer exhaustion. The light stung her sore eyes and she closed them again, burying her face once more in her pillows. For the next few minutes she could not seem to see anything clearly and imagined she might still be tied up with Freddy and his friends. Yet, when she experimentally flexed her limbs, they were stiff but not bound, and she became aware that she lay on a soft couch, not on the hard ground.

Oddly perturbed, she felt forced to concentrate again, and when her vision really cleared she was amazed to see she was in a kind of silk-draped room and against her skin was the soft coolness of fine white sheets. Startled, she stared about her, feeling she must be in some sort of drug-induced stupor. However did she come to be in a place like this? There had been a whole day of terror such as she had never experienced in the whole of her comparatively sheltered life, but the ending of it was obscured and hazy. She had a vague recollection of being carried in strong arms, of her head resting helplessly against a broad shoulder. Then there had been a voice, deep and hard, drumming angrily on her fading senses, but that was all.

Her rescuer, if she could call him that, must have brought her to this large tent which, at first glance, did not seem so very different from that other very dreadful one. She saw now that her bed was covered with a fine blanket, and on the floor around her were spread the most beautiful skins, the stripes and swirls of their incredible patterns gleaming with a satin-like sheen. There was no movement from the curtain which hung over the door, so Ross guessed she must be in some sort of inner room as the light wind she could hear outside failed to stir it.

A frown creased the smoothness of Ross's brow as her mystified glance returned to the lovely clear blue of her bedspread. Where was she? Exactly who was the man who must have brought her here? Over and over in her mind she tried to recall his hawk-like features, the cruel line of his lips, the steel of his eyes, the only parts of him entirely visible in his hooded burnous. Why was there nothing that she could remember clearly? She was only left with the impression of great strength and an even greater intolerance.

Suddenly she did remember Freddy, and her heart shook with fright. Where was he, and the others? Faintly she recalled attempting to ask the man to rescue them too, but failing to make herself heard. Was she still unable to speak? Tentatively she tried her voice in a whisper and was relieved to find it had returned. Her throat was still sore, but at least when she saw this man again she could question him as to what had happened, where her companions were.

Whoever the man was, that he could have rescued Freddy as well as herself she had no doubt. Simply to look around this tent told her he must be comparatively wealthy, and Freddy had told her that in the desert money was the greatest influence of all. Nervously she considered that he might possibly be a bandit, no better than the men she had escaped from. Could he have bargained for her—a girl, in exchange for repairing a truck? Yet she couldn't have looked anything but repulsive, filthy as she must have been from the dirt and sand.

Which brought to Ross the startling realisation that she was now remarkably free of it, there being no sign of either oil or sand on her slender arms and hands. Even her face felt clean and wonderfully soothed, the skin no longer hurting as it had done in that other, awful tent. She felt weak, oddly listless, disinclined to get up or to bother her head with the things that worried her now, but overall she was free of pain. Remembering the fierceness of it shooting through her limbs as the nomads had released her, she couldn't restrain a heartfelt sigh of relief.

A sudden sound made her hold her breath with a consuming fear. Having made up her mind to confront her new jailor coolly, she couldn't account for a shivering apprehension. It was a footstep she had heard, and with a soft rattle of rings a hand drew aside the curtain that hung at the door and a girl came in.

Ross stared, feeling a flood of relief that it was not the person she had feared it might be. This was a girl, and young, and though she was swathed in a dark-coloured dress her face was not veiled. She had dark hair and eyes and her skin was brown and smooth. Altogether attractive, she smiled. It was this that Ross found suddenly so wonderfully reassuring, so immediately calming to her taut nerves that she relaxed with a sigh.

The girl's shy gaze dropped humbly before Ross's more inquiring one. '*Bonjour, mademoiselle*,' she greeted her, in passable French. '*Est-ce que je vous dérange?*'

'*Non*,' Ross heard herself replying gently. 'No, you are not disturbing me. I was beginning to feel very much alone.' She couldn't be sure the girl understood—Ross's own French leaving a lot to be desired as she had never used it much since she had left school.

But the girl nodded, as if she understood quite clearly and was sympathetic. Ross felt a small measure of warm satisfaction. Suddenly there were so many questions it became imperative to ask that she scarcely knew where to begin. Her thoughts curiously disorganised, refused to be sorted logically. There were so many things she wasn't at all sure about. She had no idea how she had got here, for instance, nor how much this innocent-looking girl knew. It would be embarrassing, but not impossible, to confess having been tied up, in much the same way as an animal, with three friends, only she had no wish to see the first friendly face she had seen in days go cold with shocked disapproval.

Ross nibbled at her full bottom lip in considerable per-
plexity. While consumed with a growing anxiety about
Freddy, she felt it might be advisable not to mention him to
this girl. Maybe it would be better to concentrate on her
immediate predicament? If she cultivated this girl she could
be invaluable. Unless, of course, she belonged to the ruthless
barbarian who had brought Ross here? A slight tremor
shook Ross's fast beating heart. She had little doubt that
Lance had brought them deep into the desert, and hadn't he
once told her, in one of his mocking moments, that some
men of the desert still kept many women? Ross found it
hard to believe she could be in any danger herself. She was
too thin, surely, to please an Eastern man. These men were
acknowledged to like women of more generous proportions.
It was merely the strangeness of such things that stirred a
kind of primitive fear, along with the stupid suspicion that,
in spite of such civilised surroundings, the man who had
rescued her might insist on some sort of repayment before he
let her go.

As Ross remained silent the girl drew nearer, her downcast eyelids rising slightly to study Ross curiously. She did
not speak again, and Ross felt a flash of the spirit she had
thought lost for ever returning.

'I would like to get up,' she said quickly, 'I would like to
have my clothes.' When the girl frowned, Ross, imagining
she didn't understand her indifferent French, pointed mean-
ingfully at the thin scrap of silk she was wrapped in, grasping
the filmy material with disparaging hands.

'Non, non, mademoiselle!' The girl shook her head
wildly, looking positively frightened. 'Sidi ben Yussef leave
orders you must stay in bed!'

'But I have no desire . . .' Ross began, then stopped. So
that was his name—ben Yussef! The girl spoke it with what
seemed to Ross exaggerated respect. What, Ross wondered,
was his Christian name? This ben Yussef must be the man
who had brought her here. Well, she wouldn't be dictated to
by the likes of him! Restlessly she stirred. If she had owed
him anything she would have felt it. The cruel way he had
held her across his saddle surely cancelled out any need for

gratitude. If by bringing her here, and treating her for a short while like a human being, he expected her to go down on her knees and shower him with thanks, then he had better think again!

'You may go and tell Sidi ben Yussef,' she continued defiantly, 'that I have no intention of obeying any order of his. He may command, but it will be in vain! He is merely a ruthless savage. Didn't I see it with my own eyes!'

There, she decided, with a fierce inner surge of achievement. That should put him well and truly in his place!

The girl seemed visibly to shrink, her large doe-like eyes widening with bewildered horror. 'Yes, *mademoiselle*. If you request it then I will tell him,' she mumbled helplessly, backing from Ross's presence but staring at her as if she thought the ordeal she had been through must have affected her mind.

Left on her own again, Ross stirred restlessly, the aftermath of her anger leaving her tearfully weak. She didn't feel quite so brave any more. She felt sick and listless, suddenly regretful of her rather childishly impulsive words. Not that she need probably fear the girl would remember them long enough to repeat them. Perhaps she wouldn't dare repeat them to this Sidi ben Yussef? Even his name had an arrogantly repressive ring. Recalling how far she had been forced to go to attract his lordly attention, Ross could only think of him with an ever-increasing aversion.

Maybe she had been a little too hasty about the girl, too quick to send her away? It might have been wiser to have kept her here longer. The girl might have known something about Freddy? What had happened to him. With a bit of patience she might have been persuaded to talk?

The thought of Freddy, possibly still in that dreadful tent, seemed to call for immediate action. She must make some effort to rouse herself, not just lie here! It was still daylight but soon it could be dark, with that Eastern swiftness that was frightening. It was up to her to rescue her half-brother surely, but to do this she must be up, find some clothes and maybe a horse so that she might be as far away as possible before Sidi ben Yussef returned to stop her!

With an effort Ross threw back the covers of her low bed
and for a moment the lack of strength in her arms alarmed
her. As soon as her feet touched the floor she felt curiously
dizzy and was forced to sink back briefly against the softness
of her pillows. As it was only a few hours since she had been
freed from her captors she supposed it was not too surprising
she should feel like this, but it was not something she was
prepared to tolerate. She could never remember feeling so off
colour before. Unsteadily she struggled until she sat on the
edge of the mattress, her pulse, for no reason she could think
of, jerking. If it had been sounding a kind of warning she
didn't listen! All too soon she was to wish bitterly that she
had. Then she might have made an effort to get away
sooner, to have avoided any further contact with a man she
was more than prepared to detest, although she didn't quite
know why.

To her dismay, for all her tentative planning, it was
scarcely minutes later that the door curtain was none too
gently thrust aside and he was there before her.

Ross's heart gave a peculiar lunge and antagonism raced
through her body. For a moment they were both very still,
not speaking, just warily looking at each other. He was
much as she remembered him, his face hawk-like, even
handsome beneath the white *shemagh* on his head. He
appeared to be a man well into his thirties, unsmiling and
somehow frightening as he gazed at her narrowly as she
swayed weakly on the side of the bed. His eyes flicked over
her sharply, and she felt their hard impact as if he had
actually hit her.

'How dare you walk straight in here like this!' she burst
out nervously. Her voice was husky but getting stronger, if
her throat still hurt. 'Who are you?' she whispered, her
bravado changing to a sudden trembling as he did not
appear inclined to answer. She had to force herself to be calm
by gripping her hands tightly together. Foolishly she had
forgotten how broad-shouldered he was, how strong. He still
wore the burnous she had seen him in earlier and something
of the wildness of the desert seemed to cling to him as he
stood there unperturbed, regarding her coolly.

'I asked who you were?' she tried again, unable to bear the irony of his scrutiny any longer.

'My name, *mademoiselle*,' he said at last, 'is ben Yussef.' His tone was impersonal and there was a hint of firmly held restraint in the curve of his mouth. 'This, I presumed, you already knew, as Jamila told me you wished to convey a message?'

Uncertainly Ross looked at him beneath her thick lashes. Did that mean Jamila's courage had failed at the last minute? Or that, being the man he was, he was well aware of the opinion she had perhaps expressed too rashly? 'I would like to know where I am,' she muttered sullenly, 'and why you've brought me here. I don't like being fobbed off with native servants!'

The line of his ruthless jaw hardened as his dark glance pinned hers. 'If I remember correctly you begged me to take you, *mademoiselle*.' He ignored her remark about Jamila.

Ross shivered miserably, knowing it would be futile to deny this. She hadn't begged him in so many words, but in every other way. Even so, she must make it clear that that episode was over and done with, that she must leave here at once. 'That wasn't quite what I meant,' she cried distractedly, 'but if you continue to stare at me as you are doing then you must expect me to say the wrong thing!'

He bowed, a mocking inch from the waist. 'I am glad to hear, *mademoiselle*, that your insolence is no more intentional than my close surveillance. It is merely that I must continue to assure myself that you are a girl. However, this I perceive today you are undoubtedly.' His eyes, as if indifferent to her objections, continued to study her consideringly, and realising suddenly just how little she had on, Ross slid back under her silken sheets. Embarrassed, her cheeks flushed a dull red. She had never had a man look at her like this before and her heart thumped erratically. From somewhere she conceived the fleeting notion that he was deliberately taunting her, but beneath his steady gaze she could fix nothing in her mind conclusively!

He concluded suavely, 'It becomes hourly more difficult to understand how, even allowing for the ridiculous licence granted to the modern young woman, you come to be travelling as you are.'

'You find it—er—repulsive, *monsieur?*' she countered, unable to restrain a note of aggression, even while she realised he had a point.

'As repulsive as you appear to find me, *mademoiselle*.' His eyes gleamed with a mockery she instantly resented. She was in no way ready to admit that it was one thing to air her own opinion of him, but quite another to be criticised herself! She hated his hard, deliberate indifference, but she must not let his barbed words get under her skin. He was just a barbarian anyhow!

'I am English!' she announced quickly, with more than a hint of panic, which, if she had stopped to think, seemed to contradict all her careful reasoning.

'Yes,' he drawled dryly, to her amazement addressing her perfectly in that tongue, 'I thought you might be, but that is no excuse to feel superior, or imagine you have the sole right to speak your mind.'

Ross had the grace to colour guiltily, having been brought up to be polite. 'How did you guess?' she spluttered, feeling at that moment anything but superior.

'It wasn't difficult. Your truck was obviously from that country, and I noticed one or two old English magazines. I wasn't sure about you though.'

'You speak my language perfectly,' she said grudgingly.

'Yes. Much better than your French.'

That was all. He wasn't giving much away. She was not to learn how he had acquired such expertise, for his aloof air of detachment did nothing to encourage her to ask. Now that she had had a chance to have a good look at him there was something about this man that she found frightening, and fright had always made her indiscreet. 'You may go now,' she lifted her small chin boldly, 'and send your servant back with my clothes. Then I will talk to you.'

His eyes flashed a dark fire, and she was aware of a carefully controlled anger. 'If I remember correctly, *mademoiselle*, you dismissed Jamila yourself with a message—one which scarcely does you credit, and which caused her some pain to repeat.'

Ross flushed faintly, yet she kept her chin at the same defiant angle. 'I am sorry,' she retorted coolly, 'if your feelings have been hurt, but I like to be frank. I should have thought a man like you would appreciate it.' Apprehensively she hoped he didn't guess how she quaked inwardly, or what it cost her to maintain such a bold front!

For an instant his face darkened so formidably that she felt physically shaken. Had she gone too far?

'You are impertinent, girl!' he exclaimed, his tones matching the hardness of his eyes. 'I find you in a tent with three men, having no doubt received, in spite of your incredible indifference to any moral code, more than you bargained for. To escape your predicament you chose a way not many women would have lowered themselves to even consider! Now, I suppose, having achieved what you desired you hope also to escape the consequences of your behaviour?'

A fine perspiration broke out on Ross's brow as she stared numbly up at him. Her head was thrown back and her childishly silky blonde hair tumbled heavily about her slim shoulders. The impact of his temper and curt words made her feel faint again. His opinion of her obviously couldn't be lower, if she didn't quite understand the total meaning of what he implied. 'How else could I have attracted your attention, *monsieur*?' Helplessly her lips trembled and she tightened them fiercely, too proud to point out that she had been desperate.

'You have a voice,' he reminded her brusquely.

'You couldn't know the condition of my throat,' she protested. 'My voice had gone! It might be only a few hours ago and, if it does seem to have recovered, I remember clearly!'

'A few hours ago!' he jeered cruelly. 'Then you have no idea just how long you've been here?'

Startled, she frowned, retorting blankly, 'But it's not yet dark and it was in the afternoon, I think, that you came.'

His reply surprised her even more, bringing a quiver of fear to her face. 'You have been here exactly two days, *mademoiselle*. Two days in which I have wasted much valuable time, with nothing yet to convince me such a sacrifice was worthwhile !'

She was so filled with dismay that his sarcasm went unheeded. 'How could I have been here so long?' she whispered, as if unable to bring herself to believe him.

Unmercifully he loomed over her, his hand shooting out to grasp her right wrist—an action that made her cry out in surprised pain as his long, steely fingers closed over the weals left by the ropes. 'Do you wish me to show you, to remind you of the other marks on your body, girl? You have lain on your couch and been delirious almost two whole days. If my general opinion of you is to remain low, perhaps I can bring myself to believe what you tell me about your voice. Your condition when we brought you here was not good, and another few hours in that tent would not have helped.'

For a moment, seeing how he had possibly saved her life, Ross felt unhappily ashamed. The last vestige of colour drained from her face as she saw how she might be greatly indebted to him, and that he was a man who kept full account of what was owed him. His lean fingers, still on her arm, were sending warning signals to her brain, though the exact interpretation remained a mystery. A curious sensation, not unlike excitement, was making itself felt throughout her whole being. Her pulse was racing, something she never recalled happening before, and the thought of his hands removing her tattered clothing caused her to shiver all over. 'You washed me, cleaned me up?' she cried involuntarily.

'No,' his eyes went over her slowly. 'I am not particularly interested in unconscious females, even those with the body of a slender young Venus. I left the undressing and the washing, the actual nursing, to Jamila and her sister. They have looked after you well and deserve your thanks. I was, however, obliged to supervise the very necessary drugs. With their aid you have slept until the worst of the pain and shock has gone. It actually surprises me to see you so far recovered, but it is undoubtedly my duty to warn you that this could be deceptive. For a little while longer, at least, you must take care.'

Lifting her vivid blue eyes to his face, Ross saw how the light caught his profile, remote and strong, as he bent over her to examine her wrists. His voice was compelling, even beautiful, with dark velvety tones when he wasn't being harshly and outspokenly frank. He could be distinctly unpleasant, yet, in spite of this, there was the sudden conviction, even if she disliked it, that he was vastly superior to a lot of men. This, of course, she refused to acknowledge. 'You can't possibly have had any medical training,' she shrugged lightly, 'but what you have done for me has obviously helped.'

'Such generosity!' he drawled, dropping her hand as he straightened. 'But do not let your natural repression worry you. In my own way I shall extract all the gratitude I desire before you leave me. Be very sure of that!'

The soft, savage emphasis in his peculiarly threatening words jerked Ross swiftly back to reality. Whether this man liked it or not she must get up, get dressed and find Freddy. 'What about the others in that tent?' she asked wildly.

'What about them?' His broad shoulders moved laconically.

'You ask me—that!' She could have screamed at his obvious indifference. 'Didn't you send any men back to rescue them, if you didn't feel inclined to go yourself?'

His glance met hers, quite without remorse. 'I imagined they were old enough to look after themselves,' he drawled coolly. 'If not it might teach them a much needed lesson. To wander irresponsibly in prohibited areas is a habit that maybe only experiences like this will cure them of.'

Ross almost gasped. If she hadn't been so confounded she might have done. As it was she seemed depleted of all breath. There was too much to confuse her! What with being here for two whole days and now not knowing what was happening to Freddy? How any man could be as hard as the one standing beside her she could not think. 'One of those men happens to be my half-brother,' she choked, 'so I'm afraid I can't share your indifference!'

For a moment she imagined a slight expression of satisfaction flickered across his relentless face. Surely he could not enjoy the thought of her suffering over one of her family?

'How old is your half-brother?' he asked.

'Twenty-six.'

'And you?'

'Why should my age matter?'

Impatiently his eyes narrowed. 'Must you always be so defiant, girl? I require to know.'

When he spoke like that she could defy him no longer. 'Twenty,' she gazed at him sulkily, not caring for the feeling he could so easily impose his will over hers.

'Twenty! *Mon dieu*, but it is incredible! Your parents must be insane to let you out of their sight!'

Noting how his implacable jaw tightened, Ross shuddered. What would his reactions be if he was to discover she had no parents, that Cynthia had no idea she was here? That Cynthia thought she was in Cornwall with Freddy's cousin! Instinctively she knew it was much better he did not find out, and even more imperative that she got away before he ground this information from her. 'If you would let me have my clothes, *monsieur*, I would be much obliged.'

'So you can escape again, I presume?'

'Well, why not?' Unintentionally she found herself challenging his dryness. 'Though escape is not the word I had in mind. I simply intend thanking you for all you have done— then go. Obviously I can't just stay here while my brother is in danger!'

About that he made no comment. 'You would be of no help to anyone, *mademoiselle*, if you were to perish in the desert. And I might not be around to rescue you another time.'

Rashly she retorted, 'I don't believe it's as dangerous as all that. Not from what I've read. Not nowadays!'

'Books and first-hand knowledge can be two vastly different things,' he said curtly. 'Remember, too, that I came about you honourably, as part of a deal. It is a sad failing in your sex to try to wriggle out of a bargain which, on second thoughts, does not suit you. You cannot pretend you did not offer yourself to me? Your actions could not be construed as anything else but an invitation!'

Speechlessly Ross's breath caught in her painful throat. He could only be joking? Unless she misunderstood? His swing from English back to French was confusing. And she must not forget that for all his undoubted good looks he was a Berber, or a Bedouin, perhaps. One of the many millions who made up the Arab race. As such, he might not find it easy to translate his exact meaning into English. It might be wiser to ignore what he said rather than argue. If nothing else, it could be more dignified.

'I only asked for my clothes,' she murmured, with an effort speaking meekly.

His sensuous mouth quirked at the corners. If she hadn't known otherwise she might have imagined he could read her thoughts clearly, and was ironically amused by them. 'If I wanted to, girl, I could not oblige you. Your clothes are in too sorry a state to be of much further use. Unfortunately the wandering nomad whom I bargained with would not consider parting with any of your personal belongings, but Jamila will find you something, if you are patient.'

'Patient?' Ross cried, trying to hide another surge of uneasiness with indignation. 'For how long?'

'For as long as it takes you to get a good rest before dinner.' His eyes went keenly, if unsympathetically, over her white face, her gently perspiring brow, the grip of too tense knuckles on the sheet. 'You will find, when you do get up, that you have barely the strength to walk across your tent, let alone the Sahara. So do not be too ambitious, girl. Besides, you will find, in the desert, there is seldom a need to hurry.'

'No . . . !'

But he cut her down ruthlessly as she began to protest. 'You will dine with me, girl. That is an order, and I like to be obeyed, as you already know. We have discussed nothing of any importance yet. I do not even know your name.'

'Ross,' she whispered, without meaning to, 'Rosalind Lindsay.'

'Then I will see you later, Rosalind Lindsay,' he replied deliberately, as he left her.

Completely unnerved, she watched as he whipped his white burnous closer around his tall body and strode from

the room. In the doorway he turned, and Ross had to admit
he looked magnificent—if the glance he flung at her caused
her to tremble.

'I would advise you not to send any more of your so
flattering messages with the servants. They do not understand.'

That was all. He gave her no chance to reply, merely left
her to flounder in a flood of repressed antagonism, like a
concubine who had displeased him.

Ross, the flare of temper almost consuming her, tried to
get up, to run after him, but was amazed to find herself too
weak. The tent swam hazily around her and her legs would
barely support her, and she was forced to do as he ordered
and rest again.

Involuntarily she shivered, even her face feeling cold with
dislike as she lay there and thought about him. Never before
had anyone spoken to her as he did. He ignored all her
wishes, refused to help Freddy and treated her as if she was
a prospective slave! Would he beat his slaves? she wondered,
her traitorous pulse suddenly quickening despite her anger.
Beat them before he made love to them in the starlit magic
of a desert night, with only the *hamsin* whispering through
the white sands to bear witness to long hours of delight?

Horrified, Ross checked her incredible imagination, not
knowing where such thoughts had come from. Her sojourn
in Morocco must be softening her brain! The quicker she
was gone the better. If he was prepared to let her go. A
thrill, little short of fear, shot nervously through her quivering body. She could not forget the way he had held her
brutally to him across his horse. His fingers, cruel with
anger, had bitten into her soft flesh like steel. She had obviously been mistaken in thinking he could be a civilised,
educated man. In this part of the world it seemed perfectly
normal to speak at least two languages, Arabic and French.
His English could have been picked up quite easily from any
of the Englishmen who were so fond of exploring these
trackless wastes. He might have acted as a guide. His well-
bred, faultless articulation would account for it. He could be
a beggar!

Doubtfully, her temper still simmering, Ross frowned. No, that didn't quite fit. She was forced to admit honestly, if reluctantly, that he was more like her preconceived idea of a desert sheik. His arrogance was supreme and surroundings like these surely didn't belong to some rootless vagabond, whatever she felt tempted to think.

Jamila returned, with her sister this time. In her halting French she introduced her as Saida, and Ross understood that they would like to know her name. When she told them they tried to pronounce it after her, but it came out oddly from their earnest lips and they collapsed into a series of giggles. Ross, liking their warm simplicity and sense of fun, was inclined to join them, if only to relieve her steadily mounting tension, but contented herself with a sympathetic smile. It would never do for Sidi ben Yussef to imagine she was enjoying herself here!

It was enough that Jamila was friendly again. The girl held in her arms a pile of silken garments which Ross, to her dismay, discovered were intended for her.

With all the nimble grace the women of her race were renowned for, Jamila happily draped each garment separately for Ross to see, exclaiming ecstatically at the fragile beauty of every piece. 'Mademoiselle will look lovely in this,' she cried, 'and this!'

Doubtfully, while not wishing to offend Jamila, Ross shook her fair head. She would have liked very much to have known how Sidi ben Yussef had come by them, and for a moment dwelt darkly on his questionable generosity. Not caring to ask the two girls, she pleaded to feeling miserable and weak, not at all up to pleasing their lord and master by getting dressed. Especially, she added to herself, in what looked like top fashion for the harem!

The girls smiled, apparently fully understanding she found it impossible to make any kind of effort, yet she felt a slight, ridiculous hurt when they withdrew. She actually was sore and didn't feel too good, but they need not have taken her so literally! Above everything she would have loved a hot bath, a lovely long soak. Wistfully, almost tearfully, her thoughts dwelt on their shabby old bathroom at home, where the bath might be definitely old-fashioned but at least there was always plenty of hot water.

Minutes later it seemed almost like a dream come true when the girls returned with what could only be described as an antiquated tin tub. Ross recognised it for what it was immediately, though she had never expected to have a bath in one. There was one similar, tucked away in the depth of the garage at Springfield, which she believed had been used years ago in the house. Now the man who came occasionally to do the garden mixed his compost in it. He was an elderly man who took a great pride in his work. As she remembered how pleasant he was her eyes dimmed with homesickness.

Impatiently she reproached herself as she blinked, before smiling her thanks at Jamila. She had been away little over a week and there was every likelihood she would be back before the end of another. There was no rason, surely, to get so nostalgic. It would be quite a different matter if Sidi ben Yussef had refused definitely to let her go!

CHAPTER THREE

As she was waited on meticulously by her two laughing handmaidens some of Ross's doubts began to fade. She became quite certain she only needed to be quite firm with Sidi ben Yussef and everything would be all right. In the meantime, waited on like this, there was probably no harm in feeling like some Moroccan princess.

At first she stubbornly refused to have a bath, but after the girls had taken the trouble to carry in huge buckets of water she had not the heart to persist. Naturally she had felt overwhelmingly selfconscious, until Jamila managed to convey that she had worked as maid to a great lady before she had married and it had been the usual thing to help her with her bath.

Seeing how it seemed merely part of the day's work, Ross let them stay. She found she was actually glad of their help as she hobbled stiffly from her bed, and, after the first few twinges of embarrassment, she relaxed in the warm scented water. Appreciatively she lay back, breathing in the tangy lemon fragrance of the gently rising steam. She was becoming increasingly aware that many things in the East possessed an intoxicating perfume. Scents could be spicy, flowery, or a confusing, barely discernible mixture of both. Whatever it was, wherever it came from, it had an insidious effect on the senses.

The daylight had faded while Ross slept and the tent was lit by colourful lanterns with a much softer glow than electricity. The corner of the room where she bathed was dim, but the half-light was soothing, blending strangely with the lively chatter of the girls as they conversed above her head in their harmonious Arabic. She suspected they talked about her as she seemed to come in for some surveillance, but their gentle brown glances were so respectfully admiring that Ross felt she could scarcely object.

They scrubbed her all over, despite her half-hearted protests, then washed her hair, exclaiming at the bright beauty
of it as the last of the sand and dirt fell away. Altogether
Ross felt remarkably clean and refreshed.

'You enjoy Sidi Armel's bath?' Jamila smiled, spoiling a
little of Ross's pleasure. Yet her heart jerked as the girl
spoke. This must be his Christian name? It was one she had
never heard before. Somehow she liked it as it seemed to fall
pleasantly on the ears, something which many of the names
she had heard since coming here did not, although she had
to admit they usually rhymed well on the whole.

And this was his bath! Uncomfortably she almost
squirmed, then stood up quickly and climbed out. Because of
Jamila's expectant face she muttered ungraciously that she
supposed it was all right, then removed the last of their eager
smiles by complaining, as if it was actually the fault of the
bath, that her legs still felt sore.

In spite of a rather perverse satisfaction Ross was to regret
her hasty words. Immediately, as if determined to alleviate
her displeasure, the girls wrapped her in a robe and began to
massage her slender limbs. They used a fragrant oil and it
was like having a Turkish bath but much nicer, as their
hands seemed to possess a kind of healing magic. Ross, after
her first few protests, felt her prevailing tension magically
drain away, together with most of the aches and pains which
continued to plague her. She felt drowsy and boneless after a
very few minutes, and could quite easily have slept again if
they would have let her. It seemed she was floating, completely relaxed, her eyelids heavy, without a care in the
world. Vaguely she realised this could be her first real
baptism with the mystic desert, and that it was only in some
half-conscious corner of her mind that she found any objec-
tion.

'*Mademoiselle* will get dressed now?' Jamila said quietly,
gently disturbing Ross's dreams. 'You would be wise not to
keep the master waiting.'

Ross sighed, but while impatient with Jamila's fears, made
an effort to stir herself, too lethargic to voice her indignation.
Nor could she find the energy to restrain the two girls when,

as if correctly doubting her ability to make the right de-
cisions, they hurried her into a pair of filmy trousers, topped
by an even more transparent blouse. The serwals, as the
trousers were called, were light, clinging to her slender hips
and lovely, she discovered, to wear. But the blouse, although
of a beautiful colour, was heavily embroidered and inclined
to catch, making her very aware of her bare skin underneath.

Dressed at last, Ross felt slightly apprehensive about
dining like this with a man. With a flutter of slightly
bewildered lashes she pointed to Jamila's heavy woollen
caftan. '*S'il vous plaît*,' she pleaded, in her halting French,
'please, would you lend it to me?'

'*Non, mademoiselle*!' With a small shriek Jamila threw
up her milky brown hands before subsiding into another fit
of the now familiar giggles. Clinging to her own garment, as
if fearing that Ross was about to relieve her of it forcibly, she
turned and searched through the pile of clothes behind her.
Muttering loudly about not wishing to arouse Sidi ben
Yussef's anger, she found another caftan, this one of satin.
Swiftly, as if not noticing Ross's sudden frown, she draped it
around Ross's shoulders before kneeling to button it all the
way down to her feet. 'There,' she said, her face alight with
satisfaction, 'the Sidi Armel will find you beautiful!'

With a sigh Ross realised she would have to be content.
She had a suspicion that this robe she wore now was little
less revealing than the fragile things she had on underneath.
She doubted, however, in spite of Jamila's ridiculous ex-
clamations, if Sidi Armel would ever notice. He would be
too busy delivering another of his boring lectures!

With this inner assurance of his harshness somehow more
comforting than his approval, she allowed herself to be led
docilely to the other room. This dining area was, in its way,
as attractive as the bedroom, with colourful Moroccan rugs
covering the floor, and the wide couch covered with soft
warm skins.

The girls bowed swiftly and departed, leaving Ross standing alone in the middle of the room gazing about her
curiously. It was without windows but seemed more like a
room in an ordinary house. Yet the low roof and the whisper-

ing wind gave an air of intrigue to the already mysterious
aura of the night. There was eerie illusion here, will-o'-the-
wisp phantoms to haunt one's dreams. A feeling, in the
desert at this hour of night, of standing alone on the edge of
some vast eternity. Suddenly shaken, Ross found herself
shivering, bound by the same silken threads of inevitability
as had caught travellers and held them inexorably over the
centuries. Even the great sand moth, beating its wide, gauzy
wings against the smoked blue glass of the lamp seemed to
have no conscious fear of its own self-imposed destruction!
Bewildered by such distractions, Ross flinched. Where was
Sidi ben Yussef?

'Good evening, *mademoiselle*!' Even as she wondered,
there came instantly his deep, disturbing voice behind her,
seeming to add a touch of unknown danger to her already
anxious thoughts.

Wordlessly she spun around to face him, propelled more
by the vibrant command of his tones than by her own
inclinations. 'Good evening, *monsieur*...' Was it fear she
felt trembling in her throat at the sight of him?

He acknowledged her greetings with the same slight bow
of his head he had used earlier, the same interrogating
expression in his eyes. 'You are feeling better?' he inquired,
his level glance playing coolly over her colour-tinted cheeks,
the softly entrancing fall of fair hair, before continuing with
what she could only describe as detached interest down the
entire length of her body.

'Yes, of course,' she exclaimed breathlessly—anything to
break his arrogant scrutiny! Hadn't he stared long enough
that afternoon? Was it possible that because he so seldom
saw a woman in this sandy wilderness, he never tired of
looking when he did have one before him? How she wished
she still wore her old jeans! 'Jamila and her sister have
looked after me well,' she hurried on, thanking him politely,
'but it has occurred to me that I am probably depriving you
of your sleeping quarters, as well as your bath,' she finished
in an embarrassed rush.

His broad shoulders shrugged lightly. 'Don't flatter yourself, girl, that I am making deliberate sacrifices on your

behalf. One tent is much the same as another. If you admire the comfort of your present abode thank Jamila and her sister, not me.'

'I'm afraid I don't understand.' Uncertainly she glanced at him. 'You mean this was their tent?'

'No. When I brought you here it was to a plain, unadorned desert tent. The fripperies you see they managed to find somewhere.'

'And—these clothes?'

'Ah, well, that is something different.'

'But,' Ross hesitated, not knowing why she persisted, 'they must belong to you?'

'And it is a fact, also, that women like you can never contain their curiosity. Well, *mademoiselle*, I suggest you swallow it along with your dinner, and I shouldn't allow it to give you indigestion.'

Again, over the short period she had known him, Ross felt the stirrings of active dislike. She sensed it was reciprocated but considered his excuse not nearly so valid as her own. She had caused him some bother, wasted his time, hadn't he said, but surely, living as he did, his time couldn't be all that important? Never by the widest stretch of the imagination could he have any real reason to be rude.

If he hadn't any inclination to answer her merely interested query or to make any comment about her outfit, he had noticed it all the same. Ross could have sworn she had seen even a gleam of admiration in his eyes. He wouldn't confess it, though. He appeared to scorn acting as a man normally would in the company of a moderately attractive girl. Ross didn't flatter herself that she was in any way a raving beauty. Of course, by her transgressions, she must be a special case, which would account for the lack of sympathy on his part. He wouldn't believe in sparing her a few complimentary words.

Hostility naked in her eyes, she gazed at him. His heavy burnous was missing and he had on a pair of traditional trousers, like hers. They were very loose around his strong thighs but more tapered in the legs. With them he wore a shirt of fine linen, open at the neck to reveal the brown,

powerful column of his throat. This evening there was no
haik on his head and for the first time she saw the darkness
of his hair, the way it grew thick but was brushed neatly
back, apart from the crisp curls which refused to be subdued
behind his well set ears. He had a handsome head, Ross
decided morosely, and he knew it. Or, if not, there would be
many women who did. He was not a man, she suspected, to
withhold his undoubted charm if the exercising of it could
guarantee he would get his own way. Well, he wasn't
wasting any on her, which might be something to be thankful for, if indirectly.

She was not aware that he watched her closely until he
said dryly, 'If you could remove that hint of spite from your
otherwise charming face, and compose yourself, then perhaps we might eat. A cross companion rarely enhances the
flavour of any meal.' Smoothly he indicated the skin-covered
couch, waiting until she was seated before he sank down
beside her.

'I'm sorry my looks displease you,' she retorted childishly
before she could stop herself.

His sensuous mouth twisted cynically. 'As such, they don't
displease me at all, *mademoiselle*,' he murmured suavely. 'If
you must read the expression on a man's face wrongly the
fault is scarcely mine. Are you so blind that I must supply
words? Which ones shall I use? How best to tell you that
your hair is like the silver gleams of moonlight that lights
the desert sky at night, and your skin reflects the smoothness
of the finest sand swept to a flawless texture by the cleansing
purity of the *hamsin*. A mouth that could be likened to a
rose with the dew still clinging to its soft red petals, and that
your slender young body has about it the virginal freshness
of the early dawn, as yet untried. Only in the last instance,
mademoiselle, do I fear the eloquence of my flowery tongue
to have led me slightly astray. Imagine I didn't wish to spoil
the last line of such beautiful prose.'

Ross's burning cheeks almost scorched her, fanned as they
were by the mocking timbre of his cool voice. She had been
right in thinking him the devil incarnate! If for a short
while his words had held her enchanted, she derided herself

now for ever listening for one second. Flowery tongue indeed! His sarcasm was enough to wither a girl's heart! As for his last deliverance! 'You are determined to think the worst of me,' she choked, her violet blue eyes flashing dark fire. She didn't care awfully what he thought but felt strangely hurt that he should be so far from the truth. She had never been interested in playing around. She had never been interested in a boy-friend long enough for that!

His answer came, disbelievingly, as she guessed it would. 'If you must persist in leading the sort of life you do then you must expect people to jump to these sort of conclusions, and not resent it.'

'Of all the . . .' she began.

'No more!' decisively he cut her off, holding up his hand. 'Spare me another round of your temper before dinner. You have not eaten for over two days. I doubt whether you can find much more energy.'

Silently, and surprising herself, Ross subsided, her vital spirit suddenly quailing as her eyes met his. He was stronger than she, and she was more than a little afraid of him, although she would hate to confess it, never yet having met a man who could dominate her completely. She blamed her regrettable lack of courage, as she had blamed everything over the past week, on the insidious effect of the desert.

Fretfully, she glanced around. He talked of dinner, but there was no sign of it. A cloth and napkins were set on the low table before them, that was all. No sooner had the thought crossed her mind than Jamila returned with a laden tray which she placed carefully before them.

'Thank you. That will be all, Jamila,' Armel ben Yussef smiled at the girl. 'We will manage. You may send Saida back in half an hour with coffee.'

'*Merci*, Sidi Armel. That I will do,' she replied as she went out.

He caught and interpreted Ross's quick glance. 'Like it?' he asked suavely.

'My name?' he prompted, not fooled as she hesitated, as if she didn't understand.

'If it interests you,' she replied, with as much prim dignity as she could muster, 'I think it is very nice, if rather unusual. I wouldn't have thought it strictly Moroccan.'

His heavy brows merely lifted fractionally as he began removing the covers from the tray, her opinion, one way or another, obviously of no real consequence. Which, to Ross's way of thinking, seemed completely unfair, seeing how he had insisted !

The appetising aroma, however, from the various dishes sent every other consideration from her mind, and she sniffed appreciatively. 'It smells wonderful !' she said eagerly, not having realised how hungry she really was.

Consideringly he picked up an earthenware bowl and spooned into it a thick soup. 'This is called *harira*,' he told her, 'and is composed of chunks of meat along with eggs and chick peas. I think you might like it.'

'Yes.' Ross was too busy eating to spare time to say any more. She heard him say that the dish was very simple but that even in a camp such as this such things were always cooked with care. Each dish was prepared slowly and made interesting with the addition of herbs and spices. To follow there was a chicken stuffed with almonds and honey as well as nuts and raisins. She was so replete after this that she couldn't manage a sweet, of which there was a truly delectable choice. Instead she ate a little fruit, the juice dripping over her lips, staining them to a ripe softness that drew her companion's eyes consideringly.

The Turkish-style coffee that eventually arrived with Saida was strong and served without milk. After the wine which had accompanied the meal, Ross would have preferred it without sugar too, but Armel insisted that a spoonful would do her nothing but good, and she was surprised at the difference it made.

The meal had been delicious, if it seemed utterly surprising that a wandering vagabond like Sidi Armel ben Yussef should be able to afford to live like this. It wasn't, she felt sure, the fare of a poor man's table. How did he manage it? she wondered, gazing around more intently than she had done previously. Did he plunder the caravans of the rich, ravage and steal that he might live like them? He was something of an enigma, this rough, mysterious son of the desert who could change like the flash of an Aladdin's lamp into a disturbingly sophisticated stranger.

It was while her darkened gaze lingered so closely that she noticed for the first time how the two first fingers of his left hand appeared to have been badly crushed. It was not immediately apparent as the skin over the slightly misshapen bones was healed and perfect. If it had not been for the stiff way he placed them around his coffee cup they would not have drawn her attention.

Startled beyond caution, she exclaimed, 'You've hurt your hand!'

He said nothing for several minutes and knowing he must have heard, she had a feeling she had transgressed. 'I'm sorry,' she whispered, 'I didn't . . .'

'Stop to think,' he cut in mildly as she floundered with some confusion. He spoke calmly, but she saw the tightening angle of his jaw. 'I had an accident,' he continued, 'but don't bore me by asking when and how. It's a long time ago and something I prefer to forget.'

'But you can't just . . .'

This time he ejaculated sharply. 'Miss Lindsay!'

'Oh, very well!' She knew it was ridiculous to speak so petulantly in her position. It showed an even greater stupidity to resent his rejection of her sympathy. She realised the possibility of their being friends was remote, but surely they need not part as enemies! Every time she felt they were drawing a little closer he repulsed her, as if the obstacles between them were too great ever to be overcome. He was prepared to be reasonably cordial while they discussed the weather, that was all!

Mulling over this morosely, she accidentally caught an ankle with the upturned toe of her gold babouche and, inadvertently, her face whitened.

'It still hurts?' With the eagle-like sharpness she was coming to know, he caught the flicker of pain in her clouded eyes. 'Where the rope bound you it left quite a weal. I'd better have a look.'

Reluctantly, because he had been so abrupt over his own

injuries, Ross lifted a slim ankle for his inspection. He took
it closely in both hands and she felt a fire from his fingers
travel like lightning through her veins. Involuntarily she
gasped, and hearing it he snapped, 'So even the touch of my
bent fingers disgusts you, *mademoiselle*! If you find this
repulsive then you must learn to curb your childish reactions.
Your spoilt disregard of another's feelings disgusts me! Perhaps it would prove a just lesson to feel these same fingers
exploring other, more intimate parts of your body. How loud
would you scream then, girl? You are perhaps so proud that
no hand less than perfect has ever been allowed to explore
such delectable curves!'

His eyes scorched her no less than the flame from his
fingers and wildly she jerked away. That any man had ever
spoken to her like this, let alone touched her intimately with
any kind of hand at all, Ross could have instantly denied.
Oh, it was not that she had never thought of it, but she had
always felt that any pleasure from such an experience would
only be possible if instigated by love. And love being an
emotion she had personally no proof of, she had contented
herself with the odd, faintly questioning daydream. Certainly
she had never indulged in the kind of petting Sidi Armel
seemed to have in mind. This, in spite of odd surges of
curiosity, she had resisted, to the extent of being occasionally
thought frigid by would-be suitors. Never before could she
remember a reaction like the one she had felt when Sidi
Armel had first picked up her ankle.

Broodingly, antagonism stiffening every responsive nerve,
she watched as, evidently pocketing his tight-lipped disapproval, he examined her still livid bruises. His eyes had
lashed her as his tongue condemned her, but she was sure
she had not deserved it. Again she found herself puzzling as
to what sort of man he actually was, where he had come
from. In England she was sure no man would dream of
being so outspoken, no matter what they might think. This
Armel ben Yussef evidently considered he could say what he
liked, a licence that went with his own particular kingdom.
He appeared to regard himself as a king, an arrogant

director of these wastelands which bred a certain lawlessness into a man.

It was, in some ways, a small grain of comfort to know he was over-sensitive about his slight deformity, which seemed to have grown out of all proportion in his eyes. It amazed her that a man of such undeniable strength should have one spot so vulnerable, should still be so sensitive about something that wasn't really noticeable. He hadn't spoken again, but she still felt the sting of his cruel words and she supposed he considered it was now up to her to break the uneasy silence? Her own temper still smouldering, she didn't feel inclined. It was only a thought of Freddy, what Sidi Armel could do for him, that brought a few reluctant words to her lips.

'I think you misjudge me. When you first touched my ankle I felt an unexpected pain. That was why I flinched.' Heaven forgive me for concealing the truth, she prayed, but as it was a truth she could not have explained, even to herself, she did not know what else she could have said, why the firm touch of his fingers on the bone should affect her as it had done. 'I think my nerves are still frayed,' she added desperately, as his lips merely curled. 'They could be worse than my physical injuries.'

Visibly he hardened. 'Your nerves indeed,' he muttered, openly sneering as he dropped her foot, as if he found it suddenly distasteful. 'Nerves are the last thing I thought to hear you complain of. I should have thought you had more than enough, and in cast-iron condition!'

While Ross marvelled bitterly as to how he could twist the simplest statement, he went on, inexorably, 'If you are quite finished with your fairy stories, you might find time to recall that we have much to discuss. And I warn you, I want the truth. None of your amazing flights of imagination will do now.'

How she could hate him in this mood! And she hated to think he had touched her bare foot, even that small part of her. There was a force within him she could only judge as destructive. If she disobeyed him she sensed he could derive a

great pleasure from adding further bruises to her soft body!
Never, now, would she confess that his hands had been
somehow exquisite, that while he had unconsciously mas-
saged her ankles and sore skin she had not wanted him to
stop. Her smouldering confusion too ready to flare, Ross
stared at him with a new defiance. 'There is nothing at all
I'd be ashamed to discuss,' she declared rashly, 'but I don't
see why you should really bother. You aren't going to help
me, and your opinion of me couldn't be worse!'

He actually smiled, if it was just a sardonic twist of his
mouth, as he moved away from her to his own corner of the
couch again, where he could watch her clearly. 'If we seem
to be at cross-purposes most of the time then we must each
take a share of the blame. I certainly intend trying to help
you, although I have not yet decided in exactly what way.
My opinion of you, being based on the mental picture I carry
of a girl prepared to strip herself naked in order to get her
own way, could be prejudiced, but you have done nothing
yet to alter it.'

Ross took a deeply controlling breath, the effort to maintain an indifferent front almost more than she could manage—a fact vividly betrayed by the guilty flare of colour in
her cheeks as she bit down hard on another wild denial.
Why did he keep on about this so? He knew it wasn't true,
but she would only be repeating herself if she were to go
through the whole weary business of reciting the exact
reasons behind her seemingly indecent behaviour again.

'Good!' he jeered softly, his eyes mocking her apparent
deflation. 'As you appear to be in a more acquiescent mood
we can begin. I suggest you start at the beginning and I will
listen.'

Fine words, Ross decided scornfully, when scarcely a
minute later he interrupted with a terse exclamation.

'You mean to tell me that no one, not even your parents,
knows you are here?'

Painfully Ross swallowed. She still felt a curious reluctance
to give any definite information regarding herself, anything
that might lead to Cynthia discovering where she actually
was. No matter what Armel ben Yussef might think she

must continue to deceive him. 'No one knows where I am,' she mumbled. 'I didn't tell anyone as she—I mean they still think I'm too young to be allowed far on my own, even with Freddy.'

He said curtly, 'And have they been proved wrong?'

'Not exactly,' she felt forced to admit. 'You must remember, though, that accidents can happen to people on their very doorsteps.'

'Even inside the home, I agree, but not of this kind, I'm thinking,' he rejoined dryly. 'They probably realised how extremely irresponsible you are.'

'I don't see what this has to do with the fix my brother's in,' Ross hedged, resenting the way he could make her feel around ten years old. 'Surely I don't have to account for everything?'

'If you want my help you do!' His voice contained an indisputable authority. 'So, to start with, no one has any idea where you are? Apart from the so admirable Freddy.'

'Sometimes it's better that people don't know,' she cried crossly, because perversely she suspected he would enjoy putting the worst construction on anything she did, no matter how innocent. 'If you must know, I'm supposed to be in Cornwall with Freddy's cousin Avis.'

'A deceitfulness planned to the last detail.' His cold tones expressed all he left unsaid. 'What, might I ask, did you use for money, as I believe you mentioned you are still living at home? If you have no occupation, did you borrow from someone who had perhaps no idea either what you were up to?'

Ross hesitated, reluctant to give the true details of her job or to tell him about her savings, how Freddy had used them. It probably wouldn't sound right, and if he was to think the worst of Freddy he might never even consider helping him. 'No,' she admitted at last, 'we did have our own money.'

'And the other two men with you?'

'They came out here with the truck. They met Freddy and me at the airport.'

'Had you ever seen either of them before?'

'Why, no, but they're friends of Freddy's.'

'Notorious ones,' he grunted, 'if my eyes didn't deceive me.'

She gave a short jerky laugh. He might have expressed her own conclusions. Not that she would admit it! 'You couldn't know them?'

His face closed up on her coldly. 'Indeed I could—but that is another matter. How did your half-brother persuade such men to take you along?'

He didn't, she almost confessed, stopping herself just in time. Why should she feel forced to disclose that Freddy had only taken her along as she had provided the money? Why should this man know she was like a stray cat whom nobody particularly wanted? 'I was to be cook. In fact I did do the cooking,' she replied, her small chin tilting to his sceptically raised eyebrows.

'You took your time about that. As if reluctant to state your true role!'

'What do you mean?'

'I mean—men like that don't have cooks. They do often have women along, but that was certainly never their original name.'

'Why . . . !' Ross could have scratched her fingers down his scornfully ironic face! 'They never so much as tried anything—at least . . .'

'At least . . . ?' His eyes narrowed to points of steel. 'Do continue, Miss Lindsay. I detect scarcely the hint of a blush and you don't need to spare mine. You might find I'm almost as broad-minded as you are.'

It infuriated Ross even more than he did to find her cheeks growing unnecessarily hotter. 'I hadn't anything more to say,' she burst out impetuously.

A strange expression crossed his tanned face. 'What an insolent child you are! But at least when it comes to lying you aren't very adept. Don't you realise you're condemning yourself with nearly every other sentence?'

'Because you choose to apply the wrong construction. I may well accuse you of having already judged and condemned me, on your own evidence, not mine!'

'Very well,' his firm lips relaxed but just a fraction, as he agreed suavely, 'I am prepared to listen while you tell me what you were all doing so far into the desert. Your companions must have known that some of the frontiers are closed.'

'They, I mean, Freddy told me . . .' Ross hesitated, never having felt so miserably mixed up. It couldn't be any offence to look for something someone else had abandoned. Should she tell him? Well, why not? 'It was somebody's gold,' she began cautiously, 'that had been lost since the war. It was supposed to be in Tunisia or Libya, but Lance—he was the elder of the two other men—had a theory that it could be in some other place. Anyway, they were trying to find it. I didn't know about this until it was too late to turn back.'

'Good God!' ben Yussef's face was incredulous. 'Not that old story again! It's something people have been searching for for years!'

'And never found?'

'It probably doesn't exist, but gold, any gold, has always been a fever in man's blood, and these lands have had their fair share. When the lust for it gets hold of a man he will stop at nothing. Did you never consider this, little fool?'

Ross trembled, though she didn't know why. She couldn't even find it within her to be mad at what he had just called her. 'I told you,' she whispered, 'I didn't know!'

Resignedly he shrugged, as if this must suffice. 'When did you run into the—er—nomads?' he asked abruptly.

She suspected he knew more about the identity of the men who had captured them than he admitted, but felt suddenly too weary to probe. Instead she said meekly, 'The day before you found us.'

He frowned sharply. 'You were in a pretty bad shape. Yet your half-brother and his accomplices seemed fairly well?'

'It was because they had been given something to eat and drink, and not bound so tightly. I was given nothing, although the boy who brought the meals seemed occasionally to take pity on me and wet my lips.'

Ben Yussef's mouth clamped on a half uttered oath as she continued in a matter-of-fact way, 'They didn't know I was a girl, you see. Lance annoyed them and they immediately tied

him up. Then they wanted the truck and insisted that
Freddy and I got it going. When we didn't succeed they tied
us up too. Lance said—or was it Freddy?—that he suspected
they hoped I would die of natural causes as I was too thin
and small to be of any use.'

The eyes of the man beside her flicked the full curve of
one profiled breast sardonically before he replied. 'You realise what could have happened to you if they'd known you
were a girl? Many tribes roam these deserts. Even today
many are barely civilised, at least not as we understand the
word. They are usually extremely honourable, but often
beyond the control of any government—if one could ever
ascertain exactly which government they belong to. They slip
over frontiers like shadows in the night, impossible to pin
down, gone before morning. Their women are usually veiled
and protected before strangers. This is probably why they
didn't question your disguise, but you could have been taken
and never seen again. Can you not imagine the anguish of
any parents who know their daughter to be missing under
such circumstances?'

'I didn't intend to worry anyone,' Ross gulped, feeling the
full lash of Armel ben Yussef's words. She felt so badly
about it now, she could have wept. But not before this man.
Never in front of him! He was so without understanding he
would more than likely just laugh at her tears. 'If you could
only help me to find Freddy,' she hated even to plead, 'then
I'll swear I'll go straight home!'

'But that you won't do,' he astonished her by exclaiming,
his eyes still smouldering. 'I think it's quite time you were
taught a sharp lesson—a well deserved one, I might add, one
your parents are either unable or unwilling to provide. I
should be little less than irresponsible should I let you go just
yet. To come out of this unscathed with merely a sneer of
youthful triumph on your lips!'

'What . . .' Far from being triumphant, Ross shook so she
could scarcely form a simple sentence. In this mood Armel
ben Yussef scared her, terrified her, in fact, much more than
even her previous captors had done! 'What,' she stammered,
'do you intend doing with me? Surely you must realise you

can't keep me here? I wonder that you appear to consider yourself honourable!'

Although she knew she had spoken unwisely she wasn't quite prepared for his fury.

'*Mon dieu!*' For a moment he went completely still, like some lean marauder of the jungle ready to pounce, 'you amaze me, girl,' his eyes scorched her. 'You play noughts and crosses with every danger one can think of and expect to escape untouched! What will happen next time unless you have something to make you pause and think? I would be rejecting my duty to society to allow you to return exactly as you are!'

She tried to fight back, filled with a fierce desire to battle wildly against walls which seemed to be closing in on her. But the weariness within was consuming her now, drowning her rising tide of anger. She could only whisper, 'You can't keep me here, a virtual prisoner! If you do then you will be no better than the nomads you saved me from!'

'Just so long as you acknowledge I did save you, you can stop worrying about any stigma on my character.'

Pausing, Ross attempted to move him with persuasion. 'With the men you must have, surely you could have dictated to those rogues?'

His lips thinned, as if he shrewdly recognised her desire to deviate. 'I had three men with me that day. The nomad had not less than twenty—scarcely a number to be argued with, especially as I happened to be unarmed. He offered you—if I could repair the truck, and you, in turn, offered what I correctly assumed was yourself. Do you not then believe, as I asked you before, in keeping a bargain, girl?'

'But that was simply your own construction! You know I only begged to be rescued. If I could have escaped another way, don't you think I would have done so? What you have in mind is clearly ridiculous!'

His derisive smile mocked her. 'What exactly do you imagine I have in mind, girl? Is it not, perhaps, just what you desired for yourself when you first came to this part of the world? Were you not seeking a little light entertainment, a little romance to cheer an otherwise dull existence?'

'My—my life wasn't dull . . .'

'Ah, so at last you admit it!'

'Please!' Hopelessly Ross turned away from the enigmatic satisfaction on his face. He twisted everything she said, always returning to the same conclusions. Why was he so determined she should suffer for a licentious life she had never led? Gazing at him again, she shuddered, wondering instinctively what kind of dangerous bitterness drove him. Could it be a sudden anger against a fate which left the fingers of an inferior person like herself unblemished while choosing to rob him of a similar perfection? 'Please,' she repeated, as the tent in some crazy fashion began swinging around her, 'it doesn't seem to matter any more what happens to me. If you would only rescue my brother, you can do what you like. This I promise. You see, he is the one whom —er—someone at home really cares about. If anything should happen to him it could just about break her heart!'

CHAPTER FOUR

For the next two days Ross saw no sign of Armel ben Yussef and for the length of that time she fretted accordingly. He had gone quickly, without so much as bidding her farewell, when she might have had the opportunity of asking where he was off to. He had simply disappeared into the silence of a desert dawn while she had still been sleeping. It was only from Jamila that she had learnt that he was visiting a distant village, but any further information the girl had refused to divulge, either not knowing what he was up to or, just as probably, having received orders not to say.

Jamila's was a curious kind of silence, shared, it seemed, by most of the tribesmen at the oasis where Armel ben Yussef pitched his tents. After a while Ross gave up trying to glean the information from them and settled down impatiently to wait for his return.

She discovered, to her surprise, that Jamila was married to one of Armel's men and they already had one small child. Through her husband Ross suspected Jamila had learnt of her attempts to find out where Armel was, and it was obvious she did not approve.

She said mildly that if he heard about it Sidi Armel might not be pleased. 'He will tell you everything in his own time, *mademoiselle*,' she advised.

Ross doubted it. She doubted it very much! It stood out a mile that he was away on some extremely questionable business—probably robbing an innocent man of his hard-earned money, or conducting equally discreditable negotiations with those possessed of slower wits than himself. Remembering how condemning he had been regarding her own character, Ross concluded tartly that he himself had not a single virtue to lift him above the level of a common thief.

Then why, in those first few bewildering hours of loneliness, did she begin to almost hunger for the sight of him? It

59

was merely, she tried to convince herself, that he alone held the key to her freedom, and in his absence she had contrived at least a dozen feasible arguments as to why he should return her immediately to civilisation.

Not that his men, those he had obviously left to guard the encampment, ever stopped her from trying to escape. They only kept an eye on her and did not let her get too near the horses. Otherwise she was free to wander at will. Most probably on Armel's orders! He was a devil, she was made constantly aware of it. If he had tied her up again, bound her to her bed, she might not have known such an agony of frustration. To be so wonderfully free without being able to take advantage of it brought an agony of mind. Armel would know, as they all did, that with the rope burns at her ankles still hurting she would not get far across the limitless desert. Even if her legs had been completely healed she might have found it an impossible task as all she could see, whichever way she gazed, was hundreds of miles of burning white sands. Much as she wished to get away, she was not yet ready to commit suicide. Here, beneath the many palms and small trees which dotted the oasis, she must wait for Armel and hope he would be in a more sensible mood when he returned. She could only pray that his wanderings, a successful looting perhaps, might conceivably put him in a more generous frame of mind.

It was to be remembered that he had promised nothing, that first night when, with her senses wearily swimming, he had picked her up as if she had been little more than a feather, and ruthlessly carried her back into the inner room of the tent.

'You are still weak,' he had said, his eyes resting keenly on her waxen face. 'You aren't fit to travel even if I were to allow it. Rest and relax, girl, until I return. People of the West are too screwed up with inhibitions. Here in the desert, if you give yourself a chance, you can let the whole world, all the so important matters that hold you as tense as a little ramrod, slide by.'

Ross had tried to stiffen, but the warmth of his hard body holding her close had done nothing to help her endeavours.

Like some small burrowing animal she had drowsily only wanted to get closer, to rest her head forever against the tantalising warmth of his solid shoulder. Only half consciously she had whispered, 'You think you can guarantee happiness, *monsieur*?'

His mouth not far from hers, he had murmured in her ear, 'Why do you imagine the people here are so happy with so little, girl? If just a very few things could be altered, put right, it could be a virtual paradise on earth. One, moreover, girl, that you might come to know, if you will submit, for at least a short time.'

He had talked in riddles, finishing his few remarks as he had laid her on her bed. Half dazed, almost asleep, Ross wondered afterwards if she had not dreamt the soft, fleeting kiss he had dropped lightly on her lips. She might have been convinced of it all being in her drugged imagination if it had not been for the repetition of the sharp tremor that had gone through her when he had examined her ankle after dinner. She had stirred, murmuring incoherently, but before she could manage to lift her heavy lashes he had gone, leaving her only to struggle with her own uncertain confusion. A growing fear that while, if he chose, he could be reasonably civilised, he could also, just as easily, be exactly the opposite!

He wasn't uneducated, this she could tell, in fact she suspected he possessed an intelligence above average, but how much did that really count, out here in such a wilderness? It might seem accurate to believe that at one time he had followed some professional career which he had been forced to give up for some reason. Or possibly it was because he just couldn't resist the desert? Something here perhaps held him as inexplicably as he appeared to want to hold her. The bonds of ancestry, perhaps, that seldom completely let a man go.

Absorbed without realising it, Ross frowned. Being a nomad, and one so obviously in sympathy with his chosen environment, Armel must surely have come to terms with conditions which were less than perfect, yet about the slight deformity of his hand he seemed extremely sensitive. She remembered the way he had flinched more than his anger. It

had been then, in that split second of time, that she had
actually felt his pain. It was something she had never experienced before, a direct if brief link with a man's mind, and
even as she had shivered, it had given her cause to pause and
wonder. Now, having fretted against his absence for more
than two days, her former sympathy had slowly changed to
resentment.

Armel ben Yussef returned to camp early on the third
evening, just before sunset. Hearing the soft thunder of
many hooves on the sand, Ross was not surprised when
Jamila told her he was home and would dine with her later.
He ignored Ross's own message, sent immediately by return,
demanding to see him at once.

Ross in her tent paced up and down in an anguished
fashion. Not properly able to account for the flooding tumult
within her, she continued to prowl, the short wrap she wore,
procured by ruthlessly cutting the bottom off a flowered
caftan, flaring briefly about her long, slender legs.

'It would be wise, perhaps, if *Mademoiselle* were to prepare herself.' Jamila, clearly not knowing what to make of
her, glanced rather nervously sideways at Ross's enraged
face, offering what she seemed to consider was sensible
advice.

The way Jamila put it, unfortunately, only added fuel to
the fire. 'I don't see why—' Ross began hotly, then stopped.
It might not be sensible to let Jamila see just how bad things
were between Armel and herself. The girl had been kind
and she might need a friend yet. Jamila, she realised, was
wholly loyal to her master, but she might be persuaded
otherwise if the need became imperative. And each time
Ross thought of Armel's dark face, the considering expression that had lain in his eyes when he looked at her, there
was a movement deep down in her stomach which, in some
gripping if indirect way, assured her that escape, other than
for reasons she had immediately in mind, could become very
necessary.

'Oh, all right, Jamila.' With a rueful smile Ross appeared
to capitulate, her face composed again. 'I expect you mean
well. You will just have to excuse me if I seem cross. You

see, in my country we don't usually try so hard to please a man!'

Jamila frowned, gazing at Ross with her huge, dark eyes which often reminded Ross of a wounded fawn. 'I am not sure I understand, *mademoiselle*,' she said slowly. 'Surely if a man is pleased he will also be kind, and with a loved one he will also show how much he cares. When my husband's arms are still around me when I see the dawn creeping through the door of our tent, then I feel good, *mademoiselle*. I know he would never have held me close all night if he had not been pleased with me.'

Her cheeks pink with confusion, Ross looked away from Jamila's anxious face, pretending to examine the tips of her oddly trembling fingers. In the Western hemisphere sex was used regularly as a basis for popular jokes and often discussed without undue embarrassment, yet in the desert it seemed to take on an altogether different meaning. At least, when Jamila spoke of it it did. She lent to it a kind of beauty in the way she mentioned her young husband which moved Ross unbearably. In her secret heart she knew a sudden wildness of regret that she would never be here long enough to experience such subtle delights as described by this humble Berber girl.

Involuntarily she sighed while forcing her mind to accept only that which was logical. 'But I am not a married woman, Jamila. As yet I have never had a—a relationship with a man, such as you describe, nor found one to love.' The thought of sharing a tent with somone like Armel brought a disturbing shudder. Where would his arms be in the morning? she wondered. Not around her! Pleased or dissatisfied, she would have served her purpose and he would be gone. How many tents did he plunder in this way? How many women had he held in those strong, hurting arms—because hold them he would! His mouth was hard but far from celibate.

From a distance, alone in the soft tangle of her thoughts, she heard Jamila laugh gently as she prepared the bath, sprinkling the fragrant herbs which not only refreshed the

body but left a seductive, lingering perfume still clinging to
it.

'I know *Mademoiselle* has yet to learn of the pleasures I
speak of, but in time, maybe very soon—for such things are
written on our stars—she will come to understand more of
that of which I talk.'

'Jamila, you can't know!' Ross, determined to shake her-
self from her daydreams, scarcely knew what she was saying.
'I'm sorry,' she apologised for her abruptness, 'but so far as
I'm concerned, I think your predictions are a little crazy!
Don't people believe the worst of a girl who travels as I am
doing in your desert?'

'Not one as innocent as you, *mademoiselle*! We of the
East do know of these things. When a girl is chaste there are
certain signs, and all those lost days we looked after you.'

In an effort to hide her mounting colour, Ross relin-
quished her clothes and slid into the silky water. If she
hadn't had the last word, she could at least be grateful that
someone believed she was still without the kind of experience Armel seemed convinced of. Not that she cared, one
way or another, what Sidi Armel ben Yussef thought of her.
Soon she would be home, and she felt glad to the very end of
her bones for the sensible English upbringing that could
afford to laugh at a man like him.

'I'll wear the rose serwal ...' she told Jamila a little while
later, at the same time wondering at how easily she had
dropped into the habit of giving orders. One she would have
to get used to doing without when she left this place. At
Springfield they would laugh at the very absurdity of her
having a personal maid, someone to dress her, to brush and
comb her long hair until it gleamed. Once home she would
be able to laugh herself, but here it was all too easy to
become compliant instead of fighting a losing battle with
every perverse streak. She could only hope she didn't become
too addicted to a way of life she must soon leave behind.

Jamila passed the rose trousers, then slid the matching
fragile blouse over Ross's creamy shoulders before covering
the whole with a linen caftan which reached to her bare,
arched feet. Then she arranged her hair again, brushing it

until it fell shining and fair down Ross's slender back, glinting with what seemed almost a special life of its own.

For a few moments Ross even felt a little thrill of pleasure at her reflection, until Jamila exclaimed, 'Sidi Armel will be pleased!'

As this seemed Jamila's stock phrase, Ross supposed she should have been able to ignore it, but as always it never ceased to rankle. Sharply ungracious, she turned away, with a haughty glance at the girl's bewildered face, and hurried into the other room. Behind her the silken curtain swished crossly and a few minutes later when Jamila crept out she was left quite alone.

She was alone for fully ten minutes before Armel arrived. He could move silently when he chose, with the feet of the night-prowling panther, so that for several seconds she was unaware of his presence. When she did realise he was there she wondered resentfully why he appeared to enjoy startling her like this. Surely she wasn't such an object of curiosity that he must regard her with such studied concentration?

Suddenly unnerved, she heard herself exclaiming huskily, without any form of proper greetings, 'You don't have to have dinner with me, *monsieur*! I merely wished to have a word with you.'

His glance, resting on her flushed young face, hardened perceptibly at the cool disdain in her voice, and his address was no less abrupt than her own. 'Didn't I tell you once before not to send a certain type of message with Jamila? I do not appreciate insolence in anyone, let alone a mere slip of a girl!'

Confusingly, for all her surging dislike, Ross found herself wistfully recalling how gentle he had been as he had carried her to bed, that first night. Now—and it was maybe her own fault—he watched her as sourly as she supposed she watched him, and the softer note was gone. His voice was still velvet, dark and deep, but without the dreamy undertones of that rare material, only the alienating rasp of silk.

Rather helplessly she shrugged. 'It was important to see you as soon as possible. Surely you don't expect me to beg before a—a person like you!'

His darkly angled face was suddenly formidable, the grey of his eyes moving to steel as he spoke. 'You'll be doing more than that, Miss Lindsay, before I'm through with you! By that time, I can assure you, the begging will come so naturally you might even enjoy it.'

With careless fingers he flung off his all-enveloping burnous. Tall and vital in his spotless serwal, his shirt pristine white against the tanned column of his throat, he moved towards her, apparently finding her small, shocked withdrawal in no way surprising. 'I trust you are now fully recovered,' he drawled politely, as if they had never exchanged a wrong word.

Trying to control her still smouldering temper, Ross refused to look at him, or answer his impersonal query.

He studied her profile, then picked up her wrist, turning it over to examine the fading marks against the white skin. 'Your ankles?' he murmured, apparently satisfied with the condition of one part of her anatomy, at least!

'Almost healed,' she replied stiffly, doing her best to reject the almost relentless magnetism that was emanating from him. A remembered sensation, like excitement, threatened her every breath, causing the very limbs he inquired about to tremble. 'Please, *monsieur*,' she gulped, trying to divert her thoughts, 'my brother?'

'Whom we are going to forget until we have eaten,' he said firmly, not releasing her hand but grasping it tighter as he led her to the same low couch where they had shared a meal once before. 'I haven't eaten since breakfast, girl, and you won't get much information from a hungry man. That you should know.'

Ross, some small flicker of courage returning, tossed her fair head with spirit. 'You don't imagine it will be easier for me to eat anything at all, in such a state of uncertainty?'

His face changed subtly, 'Lesson one must begin somewhere, *mademoiselle*. You can be grateful it is to be no more rigorous than the learning of a little self-discipline.'

'Discipline?'

'Which adequately describes what very few women possess when consumed by curiosity.'

Angrily, Ross choked, 'Do you really regard it as curiosity to be concerned about one's own family?'

'It very much depends,' he quirked a considering eyebrow. 'You could be in danger of wasting a lot of very good emotion. One would perhaps be wiser to decide just how worthy a particular member is.'

'You must let me be the judge of that.'

His hand closed reprovingly over the tender slope of her shoulder. 'As you wish, *mademoiselle*, but I still insist on patience. Now, will you kindly be seated?'

Despairingly she glanced at him. The evening was still warm, and feeling suddenly stifled she groped numbly with the top fastenings of her long, heavy linen caftan, perspiration breaking damply on her brow as she wished fervently she had worn something thinner.

'One moment,' he drawled, just as she was about to collapse on to the couch, his eyes too observant on her hot face. 'Let me relieve you of your cloak. Many garments of the East are thin, but so enveloping as to stifle one occasionally.'

'No, no, thank you.' Nerves replacing her former animosity, Ross clutched her cloak closer around her. 'There are too many buttons, I mean.'

'I think I know exactly what you mean,' he rejoined dryly. 'But do not worry—I am not about to seduce you, not yet. I am simply thinking of your immediate comfort. When I begin to think of my own then you might have cause to tremble!'

Far from reassured, even by his slightly teasing note, Ross still huddled. Until, at last, on a long-suffering sigh, he drew nearer and began to undo the many buttons with his lean, supple fingers, taking no notice of her involuntary shrinking.

'The buttons of the caftan are legion,' he mused. 'One by one a man unfastens them, so that the beauty within is never revealed swiftly. By the time a man has completed his task he is already half way to paradise.'

A tell-tale pulse beat in Ross's throat as she felt the punishing movement of his hand against her bare skin, as he deliberately completed the first buttons. Defeated by the clamour of too responsive senses, she jerked wildly away from him. 'I'll manage myself, if you don't mind!' she exclaimed, rejecting his help along with the inexplicable longing deep within her to let him finish what he had begun, to hear the murmur of his voice purring deeply in her ear.

Completely at loss by the force of her own feelings, she shook herself free of him, angered by her confusing response, her breathing ragged as she put a little distance between them.

Surprisingly he let her go, making no protest even as her fingers fumbled where his had been sure. He watched until she finished before asserting himself again, easing the long garment from her without further comment.

'I feel rather naked without it,' she confessed, with hard won composure.

His eyes narrowed over her suavely, and for a moment Ross almost imagined a return of his lost humour. 'Oh, there is always a surfeit of embroidery on these garments,' he drawled obliquely. 'I expect you have worn a bikini, *mademoiselle*, without undue embarrassment?'

She did—sometimes, but she refused to go into an argument with him about that! He must be very well aware that a bikini was usually worn under very different conditions. Even so, Ross wondered if it was half as revealing as what she wore now.

The fragile front of her blouse was embroidered in silk, a fine tinsel webbing, variegated with gold and silver flowers on gauzy lustre. Bejewelled among the gilded leaves was a handsome, pagan god, his arms encircling the clearly outlined body of a beautiful young girl, adorned in golden damassin. In dismayed fascination Ross tore her glance away, her cheeks colouring as she wondered why she hadn't noticed when she had put it on. The designs on the clothes she was forced to wear were so many and varied that she often failed to study them closely. And, more often than not, they were covered by her long caftans.

'Did Jamila choose that particular outfit this evening?' Armel inquired idly, as, to escape his searching eyes, Ross sat down quickly. 'I must remember,' he added sardonically, 'to congratulate her on her taste.'

Still confused, she answered falteringly, 'No, *monsieur*, the choice was mine. But only because the colour appealed to me. I'm afraid I didn't notice the design.'

'I see.'

It was quite plain he did see! His eyes having lingered too long and too closely, and she didn't think it was merely the pattern which had interested him so much. He had supplied the clothes, though, so he shouldn't complain. Unable to stop herself, she asked with pronounced if unconscious indignation, 'I expect you are thinking of another woman who has worn this?'

His eyes glinted wickedly. 'No one has worn it, girl. That is not to say it was not intended . . .'

Such brazen honesty! 'For whom?' Ross voiced what was a righteous extension of her whirling thoughts.

To her deep chagrin he merely smiled, whatever he might have replied being lost when Saida entered with their meal. This evening there was again the spicy soup Ross was beginning to like, but instead of the usual chicken they had *boulfaf*, which Armel explained was pieces of veal or liver skewered and grilled over charcoal, then strewn with cumin. A bowl of hot sauce went with it and she found herself enjoying it. Like Armel, she realised she must be hungry. It was a dish, he went on, that was often found on street stalls, and one, in his opinion, which was better cooked in the open than in restaurants. The kebab, he told her, was a grander version of this.

Ross pondered on this while she ate slowly. The quality of the food she was given never ceased to amaze her. It might be comparatively simple, but it was always beautifully cooked and served, as if every meal received all the thought and attention of a banquet.

'It is because our women devote themselves to satisfying their menfolk,' Armel replied, when she tentatively remarked on it. As usual, Ross decided, his observation was double-edged.

Deliberately, because her heart began to throb too uncomfortably, she retorted, 'So much luxury here, while my poor brother and his friends must be receiving vastly different treatment!'

If she had hoped to disturb Armel it did not seem she had succeeded. 'Rest assured, girl,' he rejoined thinly, 'you could find it very hard to enjoy life here indefinitely! We would perhaps be forced to remove that sharp tongue of yours first. It defeats me how you come to show such concern about men who had no scruples in exposing you to the worst kinds of danger, while never sparing a moment to ask of one who saved your life if he is well. How he has fared in the burning, remorseless desert during the past three days?'

As if she didn't know only too well he couldn't care less whether she thought of him or not! 'Of course, *monsieur*, I have wondered . . .?' Her voice, she hoped, was as suave as his.

'But only in connection with your half-brother? So, *mademoiselle*, it can do no harm, and I believe you owe it to me, to devote at least the length of one meal to the correction of such a regrettable omission.'

'As you wish, *monsieur*.' Her thick lashes lowered submissively over the blue sulkiness of her eyes, Ross attempted to nibble a piece of meat from a skewer. What did he expect her to talk about? He ruled out Freddy, for the time being, but her thoughts were so anxious she found it difficult to concentrate on anything else.

'So obliging!' Armel was continuing smoothly. 'Of course, *monsieur*—as you wish, *monsieur*! Perhaps one should never suspect the honey-bee of having a sting in its tail! You can begin by dropping the so proper *monsieur*. Your French leaves much to be desired, in any case. My name is Armel. If our acquaintance is to progress we must be on friendlier terms.'

Ross stared at him, her eyes wide, this time, with bewildered surprise. 'You talked of disliking me, of punishment?'

'But I did not stipulate exactly what form such punishment might take.'

Confused, she shivered, knowing it better to ignore his ambiguous remarks. It might be cold comfort, but she was convinced that under his half hidden threats he was more civilised than he wished her to believe.

'What have you been doing with yourself today, Rosalind?' he inquired, after the small silence had lengthened noticeably. 'If you still find it difficult to talk normally to me then let me ask you something.'

Her name on his lips had a caressing ring to it that brought a sudden warmth to her cheeks, which annoyed Ross as he sounded so cool. 'I have been wandering about your oasis, asking your people questions they didn't choose to answer.'

'How foolish—of you.' He even smiled.

'Foolish or not,' she flared, 'would you have me sit in my tent all day like an unobtrusive stick?'

His smile widened. 'Hush,' he advised softly. 'It is exactly what I guessed you would do. That is why I left orders that your curiosity should remain unsatisfied.'

'Or more likely that I should have no evidence to incriminate you when I get back to a town.'

He simply glanced at her lazily, and annoyed by her own rather undignified outburst, Ross popped a sweetmeat too quickly into her mouth, half choking as a result.

'Oh!' she cried, tears starting in her eyes, as without hesitation he leant over to thump her lightly on her back. 'You don't have to . . .' she spluttered.

'The old cures are often best,' he told her soothingly. 'I'm sure I exerted just enough—er—pressure to prevent you from suffering.'

Unhappily Ross subsided into her corner. She felt, in some way, defeated. His action had been so spontaneously natural, so like the treatment she might have received at home, that momentarily real tears mingled with the others in her eyes. Surreptitiously she rubbed them away and, as if moved to a fleeting sympathy at the sight of her tremulous young face, Armel ben Yussef said abruptly :

'If you've quite finished your meal I'll tell you what news I have of your brother.'

'Freddy!' She immediately felt a wave of subdued excitement and dared scarcely move for fear Armel changed his mind. He was so unpredictable she never knew quite where she was with him. She was learning to tread warily, even to acknowledge his strange fascination, but if he ever thought of her with anything more than contempt, he gave no clue.

He hesitated, getting up to adjust the flickering lamp, or making this an excuse to draw it nearer. Ross had a sudden suspicion it was because he wished to see her face quite clearly as he talked. Saida came in but did not speak as she swiftly removed the remains of their meal from the table. After she had gone Armel put the table firmly to one side before seating himself again on the low couch.

'You'll understand, of course, that I can't produce your half-brother, like a rabbit out of a hat, but I do have a little information.'

Well, at least it must be something. Ross gazed at him fixedly, her blue eyes almost pleading, as he paused reflectively.

He looked directly back at her, into her anxious eyes, frowning slightly, as if he didn't care for her revealing expression. 'It would be senseless to try and explain how I contacted the nomad who tied you all up. It wasn't easy. I might not have persisted if I hadn't had the right incentive.'

'Incentive? You mean—good over evil?'

His eyes shifted to the lovely curve of her breast and Ross quivered as he replied indolently, as if her unconscious panic amused him. 'You promised, remember? That for news of your brother I could do as I liked?'

'I haven't got any yet!' she retorted tersely, her cheeks flaming, aware exactly what he meant. Her rash promise!

'Why the agitation? What can't you wait for?' he teased deliberately. 'To carry out your promise. To be in my arms?'

She choked on that, her heart pounding crazily. Again her eyes lifted and she stared at him, not able to help herself. The moment went on, snatched out of time, fraught with significance. He made love without even touching her, and it seemed incredible that her untutored body should respond so vividly, as if every part of her was straining towards him. Only a desert man, surely, could speak as he did. What did she say now? The only dignity seemed to lie in silence, but it cost Ross a lot to achieve this, not to fling every insult she could think of and rush out. 'I think you over-estimate a few hasty words, *monsieur*. I simply implied that I would be grateful.'

'Which is exactly what I expect,' he nodded smoothly. 'So back to your brother—and the nomads whom I eventually ran to earth. I was fortunate. We of the desert have our own ways, but I assure you they are not always infallible. It appears, after we left that day, the truck broke down again, and this time Ali released his prisoners so they might make another attempt to fix it. To sum it up briefly, they succeeded—and escaped.'

'Escaped?' Ross's eyes suddenly glowed. 'How?'

'One of your friends, Ali complained, was craftier than the others.'

'Lance, I should think. But why did he let them get away?'

Armel's dark brows lifted. 'A man in a truck might still have the advantage over horses, if he knew what he was doing, but maybe Ali didn't try very hard to pursue them. These men are not necessarily very brave. I believe Ali feared he might get into trouble with the authorities. He had what you would call second thoughts. The desert is not quite the isolated place it used to be, you know. There is the army and the police.'

'How long ago did you say this happened?' she asked.

'The same day as I rescued you.'

For a long moment Ross could only look at him. 'So I could have been with them all along?'

'You might, or there again you might not.' He didn't pretend to misunderstand. 'You were small and they didn't want you. They might simply have left you lying in the sand. I think your little act was still your best bet, *ma chère*, even though it might have repercussions.'

Of that she chose to take no notice. 'I expect Freddy has informed the authorities about me,' she said. 'After all, we had committed no crime.'

'That,' Armel rejoined dryly, 'remains to be seen. I doubt if they will be any keener than our friend Ali to get in touch with someone in an official position. Ali believes, and I'd be inclined to take his word, they have moved on. They didn't even waste a short time in trying to find you.'

'The other two must have forced Freddy to go with them.'

Armel's mouth thinned. 'You really think so?'

'I don't know,' Ross confessed, suddenly shaken out of her former relief. 'They could be looking for me in spite of what this Ali says!'

'I shouldn't bank on it.'

'Why should I trust the word of a thief? Ali didn't strike me as being a man of great integrity!'

'I can assure you I didn't rely entirely on his information, but other pieces which I gleaned merely seemed to support what he told me. If your half-brother turns up then this theory will be proved wrong. In the meantime you stay here!'

Ross did not remove her wide blue eyes from his face. 'You really wouldn't let me go? He might never find me! And if he's in some kind of trouble, he could be needing my help.'

Armel merely shrugged. 'Three questions all in a row! So I will make my answer brief. No—to all three of them!'

She bit her lip hard, swallowing a huge lump of outraged pride. Need he be so adamant? 'Couldn't you do anything to find him? As I've just said, he could be in trouble.'

'He could, but nothing his sort can't wriggle out of. Hasn't he already escaped one tight corner? I should advise you, Rosalind, to save your sympathy for a more deserving cause.'

'He's all I have.'

'Come, aren't you forgetting you have others?' Dismissing her plea abruptly, Armel rose to his feet. 'Before you get too hysterical, girl, I think we will seek a breath of fresh air. It will not only help you to sleep better but might also provide you with something to take your mind off your half-brother. We will walk around the oasis.'

Without waiting to hear whether she wanted to accompany him or not, he took up her discarded caftan, draping it protectively about her slim shoulders, while she stood gazing up at him doubtfully. 'I don't know that I feel like going out,' she protested.

'I didn't ask how you felt. I gave an order,' he said sarcastically, almost thrusting her before him from the tent.

Bitterly Ross allowed his hand beneath her arm. Didn't he realise how deserted she was feeling? If it was true that Freddy had just gone off and left her then she would be the first to agree that such callousness put him beyond the pale. But she was not yet convinced. It wasn't possible to believe without more evidence. It was better to ignore the suspicion that Freddy did not, probably never had, cared two hoots for her, that his affection was merely a great fallacy she had dreamt up over the years for her own comfort.

Armel was so tall and relentless she found him impossible to resist. Nor did she seem to have any more energy left to fight him, not this evening anyhow. Why wasn't he smaller, more like the men who worked for him? He was probably of mixed blood, which seemed often to produce the most attractive specimens of humanity. Maybe, in the distant past, some of his ancestors had married with the Spanish or French, as he had occasionally a very definite European look about him.

Lost in thought, Ross wandered passively by his side, her mind, as unstable as a butterfly, not letting her concentrate wholly on Freddy. It would be better to wait until she was in bed before contriving to plan an escape so she might help him. Otherwise she had little doubt she was a prisoner until Armel chose to let her go.

The hour was late. Arguing with Armel, she had not realised how time had fled. Already his men, wearied from a long day in the saddle, were asleep, their tents strewn like flat black blobs around one end of the oasis were quiet. The air, after the heat of the day, was still faintly warm. Later it would cool so that it was possible to actually shiver in bed, to wonder at a climate that could reach two such different extremes in the same twenty-four hours.

It was still a wonderful country, Ross mused, her imagination caught, as always, by the vastness around her. By night one was aware of the stars, the huge almost touchable glitter of them. The moon, too, possessed the same magically fey quality of light over water, and the desert, Ross knew, could be as cruel as the sea, yet just as enchanting if its mood was benign. Tonight there was no moon and the silence seemed deeper because of it, with only the stars to pierce the velvety, sapphire darkness. These, and the whispering, sibilant sands, in the motionless, limitless desolation.

In daylight the sands became even more limitless, their isolation even more complete, but there was always something fascinating to forestall any monotony. Apart from the utter fantasy of the elements, in camp there were the children, beautiful brown-eyed babies who captivated her completely. And from the women she had been learning to cook, or rather to probe the secrets of their exotic dishes. In turn she had been trying to teach them a few of her own Western customs which she thought might prove useful. It was difficult to know if she was any more successful than they were, but the happy laughter that marked their efforts assured her, at least, that, unlike their master, they appeared to like her.

Ross sighed, her lips, as if enchanted by the dark mystery around her, softening. Her sigh, only faintly discernible to the watchful man who stalked beside her, seemed to mix and blend with the length and breadth of the Sahara and to be carried away for ever on the secret, whispering wind.

CHAPTER FIVE

For a short while Armel did nothing to disturb the more agreeable tenor of Ross's thoughts. He might almost have been in a better mood himself as he allowed her to wander where she chose, his hand closely under her arm, so that she didn't stumble in her unaccustomed long skirts. Not caring that he should be assisting her like this she tried discreetly to free herself but as his grip merely tightened adamantly, she was forced to put up with it!

They had reached the outer edges of the oasis before she realised how far they had come. Here there was nothing but a few scattered trees of palm and fig, a few piles of flat, smooth rocks where the camp children sometimes played during the day. The stars gave out a ghostly glow, emphasising the long shadows and contorting ordinary ones grotesquely. Involuntarily, as she stared around, Ross shuddered, drawing unconsciously nearer Armel as apprehension caught nervously at her throat.

'I never knew such silence existed,' she whispered, feeling it might well be sacrilege to break it, that the very gods might object.

'You probably never took time to notice before,' was all Armel said, as if it was a line he had heard all too often.

'I'm not sure——' she began.

'You're not sure of a lot of things, *ma chère*,' he interrupted gently but firmly. 'You have been around, but you've gathered little self-confidence, or so it seems to me. You wander with a man through such brilliant star-studded darkness, yet you tremble! If I didn't know better I would judge you to be full of small uncertainties. You burst into conversation, as if it was a matter of life or death. Don't you know, *chérie*, that you don't talk on a night like this? The desert, whether you believe it or not, was made for lovers, it can give intense delight.'

Ross's breath had caught so deeply as to be painful. If she hadn't known better she might have suspected he was deliberately teasing. 'Is this what you have found, *monsieur*?'

It was too dark to see clearly, but she thought she caught the glint of white teeth. 'I am merely a man, Miss Lindsay.'

A man and a half! she thought despairingly. Too forcibly she felt the pull of his attraction, despite what he did, the ruthless, taunting things he said. 'I have seen little romance since I came to the desert,' she retorted, as coolly as she was able.

'And you feel cheated?'

'It rather depends what you have in mind, *monsieur*?' she muttered cautiously, wondering with a little jerk of her heart if they might be talking at cross-purposes again, that she might be phrasing her sentences unwisely.

His laughter came cruelly, low in his throat. 'My mind, Rosalind, is depressed to consider your girlish disappointment. It seeks to correct such an omission. In fact it commands me.'

Without further words, as the sand whispered around their feet, he turned her to face him, and she wondered why she failed to struggle—why, when her caftan fell to the ground and he stood staring down at her, she didn't resist him. He was like some tall virile god silhouetted against the dark glow of the horizon, and she could only stand, a bemused prisoner in his hands, a sensation similar to the sharpest excitement taking hold of her.

The steely fingers on her arms slid to her shoulders. 'Don't pretend you are afraid,' he taunted, 'I'm willing to believe only so much! Wide-eyed, slender, silky-haired,' he mused, his gaze intent on her paling face, 'you were made for love—for a man's pleasure.'

'Armel!' The expression in her blue eyes reflected some understanding of her immediate danger, but her voice was without any great strength.

She was half prepared that he should ignore her helpless plea, but not for his cold flash of anger. 'I see you shrink! You who must have known many worse men than me! Is it because the hands that hold you now are twisted? That you can't bear anything that is less than perfect?'

'No, no, *monsieur*!' she cried wildly, her pounding heart sending the blood spinning chaotically to her head.

'You protest too fiercely,' he mocked, not allowing her to finish. 'I remember another woman, one much more sophisticated than you, who could not bear to be touched by them either. Personally it did not matter greatly at the time, but it did arouse my contempt. One day, I decided, it might be amusing to seek a little—shall we call it vengeance, by forcing one of your so charming sex, who shared the same aversion as this other, to endure my hands caressing her.'

'Please!' Ross's voice shook. 'You're completely wrong! Besides, we have known each other less than a week!'

'A week, *ma chère*?' he laughed dryly. 'If you feel no immediate response, a year would make no difference. We are not talking of ordinary friendship, you understand?'

There was much she didn't understand, but, strangely bereft of words, she could do nothing but numbly shake her head, leaving only her darkening blue eyes to plead for her.

But Armel's glittering gaze met hers indifferently. 'Your entreaties fall on deaf ears, *ma chère*. Perhaps I should even advise you to save your sweet breath as you might need it!'

Deliberately he bent, and she seemed to have no breath left for any kind of speech at all as he pulled the silken top of her fragile blouse aside and brushed his mouth slowly across the soft whiteness of her slender shoulder.

Every living nerve inside her shaking, Ross tried frantically to pull away, raising her hands to push violently against the solid hard strength of his body.

He merely laughed again, his wandering mouth finding the small pulse that beat tempestuously at the base of her throat, and the pressure increased. It was not a soothing sensation. Where his lips touched, as they wandered over her warm skin, as if seeking out every heartbeat, there was a trail of fire. A flame that ran like molten gold through her veins, transmuting defiance to a soaring sweetness, almost removing her last fraction of resistance. There was only her shuddering, indrawn murmur of protest to part her wide, trembling lips as he touched them roughly with his.

Their breath mingled as he said softly, 'You storm, *ma chère*, while your body responds. Why don't you surrender? I can't be so very different from the other men you have known. A girl like you is made for, shaped for, love. I can feel it even as you struggle while I hold you.'

As he spoke his tongue moved against her mouth insidiously and she hated him for his low, evocative words, for making her want to respond in a wholly uninhibited way. 'I hate you,' she moaned, while her heart beat to distraction. 'You don't know how much!'

His left hand, that with the twisted fingers, went to her heart and he moved it deliberately over the full curve of her breast, as if determined to assess the depth of her hatred for himself. 'Haven't I just told you, *chérie*, your slender body tells me one thing, your words another. I must find out for myself!'

With sensual insistence the pressure of his demanding mouth deepened over her own, parting her lips as he relentlessly explored. Then, as he skilfully aroused dormant senses, everything dissolved into a clamorous fever of the blood. Her arms lifted, sliding around his strong neck, entwining feverishly in his dark hair, as she strove only to get closer.

When eventually he finished with her mouth she felt the edge of his hard teeth against her hot skin as he bent her back over his arm and lowered his head, but by this time she seemed to have no strength left, or even any desire to go on fighting him. She seemed to please him, even if she had no expertise to match his own. His voice soothed as he murmured softly, even while his arms proclaimed that he had no intention that she should escape lightly. Bit by bit he was drawing her along, letting passion mount slowly, if inexorably, but without any hurrying fierceness that might have frightened her. He knew exactly where to find the nerve centres that made her puny efforts of resistance something to be laughed at. Until there only remained a delight she could scarcely control.

Closely he ran his hands down the whole slender length of her yielding back, pulling her ruthlessly against the hard muscles of his thighs, his voice thickening. 'Do you realise

what you do to me, girl, you small wildcat whom I found in
the desert? Do you intend to give me a just reward for
saving you? Life for a life—a full and utter surrender! I can
promise a trip to heaven and I will take you with me.'

'Armel!' she was shuddering deeply now, through bruised
and quivering lips.

'I want an answer, *ma chère*, and immediately!'

There was a sudden urgency within him, as if something
was moving beyond his control. Her own was slipping. She
wanted only to bury herself against him and moan and
moan, to hold him as tightly as he held her. Then, on the
very verge of simply nodding her fair head, she was filled
with an unbearable virginal terror.

'No!' there was a half hysterical scream in her voice as she
wrenched herself from his arms with a strength that took
them both by surprise. 'No, never!' she cried, tears of reaction already streaming down her flushed cheeks as her
dazed glance held his narrowed one feverishly. 'You had a
nerve,' she gulped, looking away from him, 'to so much as
kiss me!'

He made no move to touch her again, but his eyes were
contemptuous. 'Do go on and tell me how much you disliked it!'

Her eyes dropped, not wanting them to betray her. 'You
don't have to take it as an insult if a girl doesn't care for
your kisses. I'm sure there are many who do.'

'Which wasn't exactly the point,' he replied, with such
smooth hardness in the voice which only a few minutes ago
had enchanted her so softly that she flinched as if he had
physically struck her.

'No!' she shouted, despising herself that he could still
actively hurt her. 'You found me, but you keep me only that
you might avenge yourself on a woman who didn't return
your love. Your fingers could only be an excuse, and you
know it!'

For one apprehensive second Ross feared he was going to
strike her. There was a visible hardening to his face, discernible even in the starlight, a sudden coldness that pene-
trated, making her shiver almost before he spoke. 'You are

insolent, Miss Lindsay. I believe chastisement is long overdue. You can be grateful I am a man of some restraint!'

Ross wanted to sob out aloud, to lose every vestige of
dignity she had and cry that she would never have thought
it. The hasty words were on the tip of her tongue when
something warned her that she must get back to her tent
before she succeeded in arousing his fury uncontrollably.
Already she had learnt that emotions could easily get out of
hand in the desert where the thing of least importance
seemed to be common sense. While she hated Armel's terse
finale it was perhaps irrefutable. Trance-like, Ross turned
and left him, running swiftly, on legs which trembled
strangely, back to her tent.

Control came much more slowly. It was only achieved as
she forced herself into a calmer frame of mind. All night she
tossed restlessly, unconsciously muttering his name while she
slept, seeing his face in her dreams, stamped with the same
derisive expression he had worn as she had left him.

She awoke unrefreshed, with the dramatic impression of
having passed not a few short hours but hundreds of years,
that overnight she had completed the painful, underesti-
mated process of growing up. Armel, she decided bitterly,
had done this to her! He called her an irresponsible child,
then treated her wholly as an adult. He hadn't spared her at
all, and the response he had sought left her in no doubt that
he had considered her quite capable, even ready, to meet his
most passionate demands.

Stretching her slender arms nervously above her head,
Ross shivered with compulsive reaction, caught in a monu-
mental despair. Somehow she must escape before the attraction this man held for her became apparent to all. Before she
betrayed undeniably that she was not as indifferent as she
must pretend to be. If only she could find someone to help
her, someone who could be persuaded—one who was not so
loyal to Armel.

There was a man, one of those who had been left behind
to guard the camp when Armel had been away. His other
men spoke to her, but kept at a respectful distance. This man
had also been respectful, but on several occasions when he

had found her alone on the oasis he had wandered nearer.
He spoke no English and only a few words of French, but he
had been insistent. Ross had supposed he felt sorry for her,
that he had some idea of her predicament. Maybe she could
make him understand? He looked middle-aged and reliable.
If only she could get through to him, she might appeal to
him.

Her head full of half-formed plans, Ross scrambled from
her bed to rush across the tent. Swiftly she poured water into
her rough earthenware basin, splashing herself all over until
the heavy lethargy of the night left her and she positively
tingled. She dried herself and dressed quickly, without waiting for Jamila. The girl's eyes saw too much, and Ross was
not sure that all signs of the previous night's experiences
were gone from her face.

When the girl did arrive it was with a message—a surprising one. 'Sidi Armel wishes to see you at once, in his
tent, *mademoiselle*. Is not the sun shining on you with the
bestowal of such a favour?' she smiled.

Ross had her own private thoughts on that which, knowing of Jamila's unaccountable affection for her master, she
knew better than to express. She contented herself with
observing coolly, 'It so happens I have no particular desire to
see Sidi ben Yussef this morning, Jamila.'

Jamila frowned at the mutinous young face before her.
Not that Ross's face did look so very youthful this morning.
It was smooth and beautiful, but it wore too haunted an
expression. 'Please, Mademoiselle Rosalind,' she begged,
'you know that when Sidi Armel commands we must obey.
Even you.'

'How very brave we all are, Jamila!' realising all too
clearly that if she refused to see him he was quite capable of
dragging her across the intervening space between their
tents. Probably, with his black, pagan heart, he would not
hesitate to do so. She had had a taste of his unrelenting
strength last night. If only she had not been so weak, so
ineffectual in her protests, he might not be acting so imperiously now.

Dragging her angry thoughts into some semblance of

composure, she followed Jamila, trying to remember that for days she had been curious to see inside his living quarters. What he could want to see her about this morning she had no idea. She did not think he was the kind of man who would pursue his amours in the cold light of dawn. Not unless he loved a woman to distraction, and Ross felt very, very sure he did not love her at all!

He was waiting for her, standing drumming his fingers impatiently on a narrow folding table which to Ross looked more like a desk. Ross's own fingers clenched as her nervousness returned. Why did her blood seem to take up the same mad beat that she had known in his arms, even a glimpse of him seeming to move her fatally? She wanted to glance around the forbidden area, to explore, if only with her eyes, but her gaze seemed fixed firmly to that of the man who stood regarding her sombrely.

'You sent for me?' she asked at last, as the seconds dragged interminably, and she thought she might drown in the dark speculation of Armel ben Yussef's eyes if she didn't take care.

'Yes,' his smile was tight with a grim satisfaction as his glance went to where her reddened lips still showed signs of bruising, and the darker shadows of a not yet dissipated exhaustion showed faintly beneath the deep blue of her eyes. 'I trust you slept well, Miss Lindsay?' There was no mistaking the smooth sarcasm in his voice.

Vaguely she nodded as if she could think of nothing that might have disturbed her slumbers. Inwardly there was a hard lump of resentment. Did he have to refer to that?

'Which was more than I did!' Balefully he came around the side of the table to stand closer. 'How long do you usually keep a man in suspense, *mademoiselle*, before you grant him the pleasure he seeks?'

A flame licked up in the darkness of his eyes and as if it had burnt her Ross felt her whole body flinch with an agonising reaction as she backed away. Her face whitened slowly and her voice was husky. 'How much longer are you going to insist that I'm the type of woman to bestow such favours?'

They stood there motionless, facing each other. For Ross it was a moment of excruciating pain—the disbelief on his face, the open contempt in his eyes.

'I'll admit,' he drawled sardonically, 'you have little experience written on your so beautiful face. Or is it that your previous men friends have left no impression? I must warn you by the time you leave here this will be changed. You won't reject my arms for ever, Miss Lindsay. I would be a fool to think so. Your response last night was something to keep me awake long after dawn crept with rosy red fingers across the horizon!'

He ended on a note of such savagery that Ross trembled and shrank. It was as if hatred and desire combined in him, and, as his hands descended like steel on her shoulders, she stared at him, trembling, the now familiar excitement which his nearness evoked rising with panic in her throat.

'If you don't approve of me, if you are so convinced I deliberately provoked and cheated, why don't you let me go?' she whispered.

His brief laughter was hard. 'Perhaps, Miss Lindsay, it is because a man appreciates a plaything out here in the desert where even the delights of solitude can pall after a time, if there is no one to share it with. A man is not too obsessed with perfection in a toy that is bought cheaply, merely made to be discarded.'

God, but he could be cruel! For no reason she could think of Ross's anger felt more like tears, the constriction in her heaving breast pain. 'You've made your point, *monsieur*,' she cried, trying unsuccessfully to wriggle from his hurting hands. She was no match for him and he did not allow her to escape, so she lifted her small chin and tried to look at him coolly.

'Now that I'm here perhaps you can tell me why the sudden summons this morning? Surely you don't need to chastise me further for my lack of co-operation when you forced your unwanted attentions on me? If I appeared to respond at all, *monsieur*, it could only have been a trick of the night. Your arms left me cold. Why else do you suppose I ran?'

If he could torment, he would find her not too feeble an adversary. Yet she prayed silently for forgiveness for the lie that crossed her lips.

Not that he looked very impressed. In fact she saw dully that his sensuous, hard mouth curled at the corners in a derisive sneer and his eyes clearly mocked her strangled little sentences. But he simply said enigmatically, 'We shall see, Miss Lindsay, we shall see.'

'Now!' Abruptly he dropped his hands and turned away, 'I will be gone for two days, perhaps three. I must warn you, under no circumstances must you attempt to leave this camp. If it was at all possible I would take you with me, but this I can't do.'

Ross did not know why she should feel so dismayed. To hide it she pretended absolute indifference. She even heard a faint, tinkling laugh come from her lips as she murmured, daringly, 'One reads, Armel, in the best novels of how the prisoner always tries to escape as soon as the villain's back is turned.'

'So that is how you think of me?'

His name on her lips seemed to jolt him a little. His voice was low, his mockery mixed with something she could put no name to.

'I choose not to think of you at all,' she retorted softly.

He shrugged, glancing swiftly from her flushed face to his watch, as if time pressed too closely. 'But you will heed my warning. You must not allow your natural rebelliousness to overrule common sense. To be lost in the desert is not an experience you would enjoy. It is my duty, I'm afraid, to point this out.'

'Your duty!' Hurt surged ridiculously at his conventional statement. 'I wouldn't have thought you were too occupied with that!'

'But you have no idea what stirs my conscience, do you, girl? It is certainly not a crazy little wanton like you.'

The need was in him, she realised, to whip her cruelly, but again it hurt. He wanted her. If he thought she was such a—wanton, what was holding him back? It could only be pride. He would have her come crawling, begging at his feet. Crying over those broken fingers which caused him such mental pain, it appeared to be twisting his character! Helplessly she trembled, seeing herself suddenly, voluntarily in just such a state of subjection. Futilely she tried to regain some calm as his eyes strayed moodily to the seductive curves of her figure which the thin material of her caftan barely disguised. Even his impersonal glance seemed able to disturb her too intimately, and she sought desperately to find a topic somewhat removed from themselves.

'Wherever you are going to you might hear more news of Freddy? He must be somewhere around.'

'He could be,' Armel's laugh grated, 'but you don't have to thrust him between us like some sort of defence mechanism.'

'What defence could I possibly need against you?' she demanded.

'I could make love to you now and you wouldn't even fight me, not after the first minute.'

Her bodice moved with the force of her heartbeats, the frightening truth of his words. Her legs felt paralysed, incapable of movement. It was only the sound of someone approaching outside that released her. 'Oh!' she cried, as she turned and fled, while hating herself for such a cowardly retreat, such an unoriginal exclamation. 'Oh, how I hate you!'

'Don't forget,' he called indifferently after her, 'that which I have just told you. Stay within the confines of the oasis and you will be quite safe.'

Later, after Armel and his entourage left, Salem, the man she had noticed previously, sought her out. The day was well advanced when, wandering at the quiet end of the oasis, she saw he had followed her. He was a small man, extremely thin, rather ragged, but with a darkly earnest expression. Ross was convinced he felt sorry for her and it struck her again that he might be persuaded to help her escape. As he furtively approached her she tried to speak to him, but unfortunately not even her best attempts succeeded in breaking the language barrier. Not even when she pointed first to herself, then the distant horizon, did he seem to understand.

Then, like a bolt from the blue, she hit on the idea of a pencil and paper. She had seen such things in Armel's tent that morning, she felt sure, although she had left there so swiftly that no particular detail remained fixed in her mind. Hastily she gestured to the man to stay where he was until she returned. At least he seemed to understand this as he squatted obediently under the branches of a feathery palm tree, obviously prepared to wait.

Ross was reluctant to enter Armel's tent again after the tumult of the morning, but as there was no one around she knew she must grasp the opportunity which might never come again. Not for a moment did she dare allow herself the luxury of hesitation. Should anyone discover what she was up to she might never get another chance.

Silently Ross slipped through the closed flap, seeing immediately, to her relief, some neatly stacked paper and writing material on the table. Even while the faint query flashed through her mind as to why he should want such things she hastily stuffed a few sheets in the folds of her caftan, along with a thick charcoal pencil, before beating an equally hasty retreat. The whole atmosphere of the tent reminded her too much of Armel, and the peculiar sensation in her throat she did not like.

Under the palm trees Salem still waited. When she recovered her breath, Ross knelt down beside him and drew a living likeness of them both on the paper. Then came two horses and the distant horizon. This was so cleverly executed that he understood right away, without the need for further gestures.

Nodding his greying head, he smiled cunningly and held out his hand. Ross bit her lip, knowing instinctively what the man was after. With even more reluctance than she had entered Armel's tent, she drew from an inner pocket the gold watch she had managed so far to conceal. This, along with a small sum of money, had been hidden in her torn jeans and no one had apparently noticed. The watch had been a treasured expensive gift from her father, the only thing of real value she had ever possessed, and much as she hated parting with it Ross felt he would have wished her to do so under the circumstances.

Salem's smile widened at the sight of the articles in her hand. Putting out his own hand, he made as if to take them, but she had the sense not to let him have them there and then.

'Later,' she promised, and when he frowned sharply she indicated with her finger the rough city she had drawn on the paper. 'When we reach there!'

After a few moments this appeared to satisfy him as his quick frown changed into another smile. Taking the charcoal, he reached for the spare sheet of paper, clumsily but clearly sketching the first rays of sun before dawn. Ross, staring down at him as he worked, was impressed by the intelligence of it, especially as Armel had told her some of the older men had never attended any kind of school. Then she recalled that Moroccan culture went back almost to the beginning of time, that many of their cave drawings went back over tens of thousands of years, telling as clear a picture of life then as if the same people and animals existed today. And she had read that in the *madrassahs*—the Moslem law and theological colleges—artists paved the way for intellectuals, that the skilled craftsmen and talented sculptor had been the most highly esteemed.

Salem's drawing undoubtedly said before dawn. How he was going to arrange it she did not know, but these people would have their own way of going about such matters. He would not have agreed if he had not known exactly what must be done. That he had not agreed to take her until he had seen her money convinced her he was not interested in her personally, that he was wise enough to realise her watch was worth a great deal more than the trouble she was putting him to. As a lone man, without a wife, he would probably, with the aid of this cash, set himself up in a small street business; in time he would perhaps be able to afford many of the comforts Armel no doubt denied him.

Ross was ready and waiting long before the appointed hour the next morning. Again she had spent a restless night, unable to suppress the despondency that gripped her now that she was leaving this place for ever. It wasn't sensible to imagine she could really feel nostalgic about a tent she had occupied for little over a week. It was even more ridiculous to feel a great reluctance to go now there was the opportunity.

Small voices had tormented her as she had lain awake, staring wide-eyed into the darkness around her. What was there actually to return to? This country was wild and in many places barren, but it was hauntingly beautiful, in her eyes anyway. She had fallen in love with it, just as she had the ruthless Sidi ben Yussef who held her. The knowledge of this, coming as it had done like a bolt from the blue, had shaken Ross so much she had nearly sobbed out aloud. It seemed incredible that such a thing could have happened in so short a time. Yet hadn't she lived through a lifetime with Armel? Didn't the world stand still, stop spinning on its axis when he kissed her? Never had she known such emotion as she had experienced then. Never, she knew, would she ever feel it again. Nothing like this could happen twice, no matter how long she lived.

Temptation was almost irresistible. Shouldn't she stay, take whatever crumbs Armel offered, whatever his opinion of her? There could be several weeks of breathtaking happiness to set against the rest of her life, which might stretch as empty as the desert before her.

But it was the reminder that she would have the rest of her life to live that finally decided Ross she must go. She loved Armel desperately, and while he didn't have any affection for her, she was aware he wanted her rather badly. Remembering his arms, the feeling that could rise so dangerously between them, Ross realised she might not easily escape the consequences of such a possible union if she stayed. He was a man who would take all or nothing, one who wouldn't stop until he had taken every last reserve, until she was committed to him fully in every possible way. Then she would be cast aside, a man so cruel he wouldn't give her a second thought, and she could be left with two to fend for. She, who had barely enough resources to look after herself.

No! Although the ultimate outcome held a strange, almost irresistible fascination, it was one she could never sensibly contemplate. She must go!

An hour later she was riding swiftly away from the camp with Salem by her side. The horses were not Armel's best, but they had a heartening turn of speed. Ross hoped it would be possible to return them later. While she did not mind so much about bribing Salem, she had no great wish to be thought a thief.

With some difficulty she had retrieved her discarded trousers. Although they were terribly torn at least they would be more comfortable to ride in than any of the clothes Jamila had given her. About Jamila she refused to think, realising that the girl, along with others, would probably receive the barbed edge of Armel's tongue when he arrived home and found her gone. Where was he? she wondered, as she gripped the saddle tightly with her knees. Fervently she hoped she and Salem would not bump into him before they managed to reach safety. An area of this size was just the unlikely place where such a thing might easily happen, whereas in a square mile one might wander all day and never see a face one knew.

How Salem had managed to avoid arousing the suspicions of the other men at the oasis, she couldn't tell. To have done so, especially when he had had to take two horses, proved he must be cunning as well as daring. When Ross spared a moment to think of this it made her curiously uneasy, but it was something she refused to dwell on. Salem might not be too trustworthy, otherwise he would not have been so eager to desert Armel, but she was in no position to pick and choose. Salem was not anything she could not cope with. Even if the worst did happen and he ran off with her money, she would still have a horse, and she could not be so very far from civilisation.

Some time later Ross came to realise bitterly that, so far as riding went, she was very much out of practice. She hadn't, in fact, ridden since she left school, when the orphanage had arranged holidays for the children who had no one to go to. She had spent three weeks with a family who owned a riding

school, and in that time she had learnt a great deal, many of
the basic principles. With Cynthia, of course, there had been
no opportunity to further that brief education, but Ross had
thought it would simply be a matter of taking up where she
had left off. How mistaken one could get, she was only just
beginning to learn. Long before midday she was sore and
throughout the remainder of the day, which seemed the
longest she had ever spent, it became a matter of severe self-
discipline to stay in the saddle. The sun burnt her shirt-clad
back, for she hadn't been able to find a thick burnous, such
as the men wore, and her head ached from the constant
glare, the fine particles of sand blown from the hooves of the
leading horse.

They stopped only a few minutes for a break at lunch
time. Food was something Ross had decided to leave to
Salem, imagining he would understand she had no means of
getting any herself. To her dismay he appeared to have only
one goatskin of meal and another of water and did not seem
at all keen to share even these meagre rations with her. He
did, with a toothless grin, draw a handful of dates from a
greasy pocket and offer Ross these, but she felt so secretly
repulsed by the dirt on his hands that she was forced to
decline. She did manage to beg from him one small drink of
water, and with this she forced herself to be content. It could
not be for long, and she willed herself to forget her terrible
thirst, her growing hunger and remember those awful hours
she had spent with the nomads, when she had been given
nothing to eat at all.

That afternoon the charm of the desert seemed rapidly to
disappear. Instead of the undoubted beauty, Ross's mind
started to become obsessed by all that was terrifying—sand-
storms, the possibility of getting lost, of wild animals and
snakes. Of these Lance had used to reel off the names of a
few, the cobra, the horned viper being, he had said, the
worst, with the victim having about one minute to get the
proper anti-toxin. Then there was the scorpion, which had
featured so frequently in the beds of the unwanted in ancient
tales. Ross shuddered to think of the awful fate that might
await her if she did not take care.

Yet disaster, when it came, was not in the guise of snakes but through her horse. It went lame soon after the sun had reached its height, and Salem's fury was not pleasant to see. When he stopped to inspect the animal's foot he simply snarled at Ross when she tried to ask if it was going to be all right. It was clear he understood what she was getting at, if he couldn't understand her stumbling French. Sullenly he shook his head, but seemed to accept that they could now go only at walking pace while the horse still limped. This did not prevent him from attacking the poor beast every now and again with a stick, much as Ross tried to prevent it. She felt so sorry for the horse she would gladly have walked, but each time she started to dismount Salem flew into an even greater temper. Long before they halted for the night Ross was near to hating him—and hating herself more for ever having left the safety of Armel's camp.

The place where they had stopped filled Ross with further dismay. It looked like a small oasis but was really no more than an almost dried up water hole surrounded by a few stunted trees. There didn't seem enough wood of any kind to light a fire, which she knew to be almost essential in the desert.

No fire, no food, and a man she instinctively did not trust for company! How Freddy would laugh at her stupidity when she found him. Rather desperately she slid her stiff, weary limbs from the horse and began to gather up the few pieces of twigs and sticks she saw lying on the stony sand. Salem did not seem inclined to do more than watch, as if he knew the wood she gathered would only burn for perhaps an hour, no longer.

The horses had slaked their thirst in the brackish water, but dry as her throat was, Ross shrank from the black, evil-looking colour of it. Never had she expected to feel so miserable! The headache which had begun earlier now pounded, and despairingly she gazed around for some place she might lie and rest. Darkness had come, as it always did, with a frightening suddenness, and she could find little reassurance in the few flickering flames she had managed to drag from the fire.

CHAPTER SIX

Ross, her heart pounding with shock, stared numbly at the smirking, determined man before her, trying desperately not to let him see her fear as she stubbornly shook her head. It was only as he stepped nearer that her courage failed, and reluctantly she drew the precious watch from her pocket along with the money. What could be the use of quibbling? He was wiry, much stronger than she. She would rather do anything than risk being touched by him!

As soon as the watch lay in his hands she had thought he would leave her and disappear into the desert. To her horror he did nothing of the sort. After placing his loot carelessly beside his goatskin containers he turned back to her again, laying his dirty hands on her, leering at her as he tried to draw her closer.

Ross gave a scream of terror, then started to fight him with every ounce of her strength. Her resistance seemed to take him by surprise, but he was strong and she knew that gradually she was being overpowered. Her shirt tore, ripped down her shoulder and arm by his scrawny fingers, and she could hear the breath hissing evilly between his coarse lips. Wildly she swung around, pushing against him, but he gave no sign of weakening and she felt his hands closing tightly over her neck.

Then, just as a wavering darkness began mercifully to take possession of her senses, she was free. Salem was torn away from her as hands grasped him roughly, throwing him angrily some yards across the sand.

Ross scarcely needed to look to see that her rescuers were Armel ben Yussef's men. As she sank helplessly to her knees she lifted her tumbled head to see through a blur that he stood only a few yards away, a whip in his hand.

'No!' she cried impulsively, lifting both arms to shield her face, thinking he intended using it on her. 'Please,' she whispered, 'no, not that!'

But it wasn't herself he had in mind—not then. Ruthlessly, as the men dragged the cringing Salem from her, Armel's whip rose and fell several times on the man's back, and each time Salem screamed with fright. Armel seemed to know exactly what he was doing and, Ross thought hysterically, his men looked quite disappointed when he stopped, too soon to have done any real damage. Salem was lifted, flung over his horse, the animal receiving a slap just sharp enough to cause it to gallop swiftly off into the desert, a wildly bewailing Salem clinging to its back. Ross's watch lay where he had placed it on the goatskin.

Ross still crouched where she had fallen, watching Armel helplessly. Would it be her turn next? Never had she seen his face so cold; it was even more forbidding than that first time she had seen him in the nomad's tent. Ignoring her, he wrapped his whip before striding towards her horse, bending, as the animal limped, to examine its leg. There was only a minute before he straightened, then taking a small revolver from his pocket he passed it to one of his men, rapping out some low-voiced instructions as he did so. Quickly the man led the injured horse from sight and there was barely another minute before a shot rang out.

Almost at the point of collapse, Ross felt sick, so disgusted with men in general she could scarcely bring herself to look at Armel even though she owed him so much. As he came to her at last, she cried, 'Did you have to do that? Salem is a beast, but I thought you were better!'

'Indeed, madam!' his voice rang like steel, lashing her as surely as if he had used his whip. 'So we are all one as bad as another—an opinion I will recall at some future date. That horse could not have made the journey back. He never had any hope of recovery. It was better to put him out of his misery without further delay. Would you have left him to suffer?'

'And Salem?' she mumbled drunkenly, realising the truth of what Armel said. She hadn't intended asking about the man. Certainly he was horrible, but perhaps it was not his fault he had acted as he had done. Hadn't she bribed him with something he couldn't resist? Armel knew this as his eyes had dwelt comprehendingly on Ross's money and watch. What would happen to Salem now?

'Did you have to use your whip?' she breathed.

'What would you have me do?' Armel's voice ripped into her. 'Take him hundreds of miles to the nearest town, lodge a formal complaint with the police? Attempt to explain your part in the matter? By the time they dealt with him he would have forgotten the crime of which he is guilty. No, girl. Justice in the desert might be rough, but it serves its purpose very well. Salem will think twice before he commits the same crime again. Not that I am sure whose crime is greater, yours or his!'

'It was my fault, *monsieur*.' Confession might be good for the soul, but it hurt.

'Of that I have no doubt,' he retorted, his face suddenly livid as he grasped her by her arms, pulling her savagely up to face him. 'Didn't you realise—don't you ever stop to think, you little fool, what you were doing? He could have killed you, left you to die. No one might have found more than a few bleached bones!'

A wave of horror hit Ross again and she would have fainted if he had not caught her to him. Once again he called curt orders to his men and almost instantly she was lying on a pile of warm blankets beside a fire which seemed to be blazing miraculously. Armel knelt by her side, pressing a silver flask of brandy to her shaking lips.

It ran down her throat so that she choked and cried out in pain as it burnt her dried lips. Yet such pain seemed nothing compared with the one in her heart as his hard, unrelenting face swam above her. 'Armel,' she pleaded, there being no room left for pride, 'I'm sorry to have caused you so much trouble. Will you forgive me?'

As she tried to focus her sore eyes he forced her to take a little more brandy. He had removed his thick burnous to wrap around her and his thin shirt lay open at the neck, but he did not seem to feel the cold. He considered her urgently worded plea no more than briefly, and his answer brought no comfort.

'The main fault was probably mine,' he said grimly. 'Mine for trusting you. I would perhaps be well advised to give you a taste of the same punishment as Salem received. Why should I forgive you?'

'You wouldn't dare!' she gasped, all thoughts of reconciliation smothered immediately with indignation. Wildly she stared up at him, 'You wouldn't be so uncouth as to—as to . . .'

'Take a whip to a woman?' he supplied the words she could not bring herself to utter. 'I could, and I yet might, my girl, so you have good reason to cringe. Don't imagine you are going to escape so lightly. Don't you think you deserve to be punished for what you have done this day? I have lost two good horses, and a man, who while not up to much, was useful. What can you offer to put in their place?'

Ross, completely exhausted, was not able to reply. Her heavy lashes fell despairingly on her cold cheeks and stayed there. She slept until the moon had risen sufficiently to allow them to travel. Armel ben Yussef carried her to his horse, reclaiming his burnous which, once he was mounted, was entirely adequate to cover them both.

His huge Arab stallion would have terrified Ross on any other occasion, feeling as it did about ten foot tall. 'Where are we going?' she protested feebly, in no way eager to leave her warm bed by the fire. She had been comfortable and her body still ached too much to appreciate being disturbed.

'Back to camp,' Armel replied shortly, giving the necessary commands to his men before drawing her closer and tightening the reins. 'We are not so far away and my men are weary. They will be happier in their own beds.'

Not one word about her comfort, not one note of tenderness in his low but perfectly audible voice. Wearily Ross rested against him, sliding her arm around his wide waist to balance herself as the horse broke into a swift canter. She took a strange comfort from the hard beat of his heart beneath her cheek, but her own heart burned with a kind of

hopeless resentment. What use to be so near to him physically if they were miles apart in spirit? Remembering how he
had threatened before she had fallen asleep, Ross shivered.
Surely he could not have meant what he said? Yet what did
she really know of him, or the way that women were treated,
here in the East? She and Armel might appear to have much
in common, but they were from different parts of the
universe. There must be plenty of truth still in the old saying
of East being East and West being West, otherwise it would
never have survived so long. Armel and she were from
entirely different cultures and it would be crazy, because of
some strange magnetism between them, to pretend otherwise.

Unhappily she stirred. Close up to him like this, her
nostrils were assailed by the clean, masculine scent of his
warm skin, her senses by every slight movement of his
powerful body. Feeling her tremble, he said roughly, 'We
will be home in a very short time, girl. Then you will soon
feel quite yourself. Or almost!'

Would she, ever again? Although her mind shied away
from the two enigmatical words he had tacked on at the end,
she doubted she would ever feel herself, not even if she lived
for another thousand years. 'How can we be so near the
camp?' she asked fretfully. 'Salem and I travelled all day.'

'After your horse went lame Salem must have realised he
could never make the oasis he originally intended, so he
simply circled back to the one where we found you. His
intentions were obvious. He would have left you there and
gone on alone in the morning.'

Unhappily Ross sighed, her mind shying away from such a
possibility. Instead she pondered slowly, 'So you just
stumbled across us accidentally?'

'Not exactly.'

'Then—how?'

'This curiosity of yours, girl, will land you in real trouble
one day! I will just say that for once I allowed myself to be
persuaded by my instincts. I felt there was something wrong,
if not directly connected with you. It was an impression so
strong that instead of making for my next place of call, I

decided to return. If I had gone all the way back to camp I doubt if I would have been in time to save you. But by the will of Allah it seems we were meant to cross the track of your two horses. One being lame, I decided, in spite of my men's obvious disapproval, to follow my hunch. You are aware of the rest.'

'You were only just in time.' Ross's voice shook. 'Or perhaps it would have been better to have left me to my fate.'

'And spend the rest of my life, *mademoiselle*, remembering your white body lying crushed and broken!'

'Yet you seem to regret having saved me?'

His smile above her head was grim. 'You want me to assure you I couldn't live without you?'

'No!' her voice was wild.

'I would like to tell you to put this incident from your mind, but it could prevent you from committing the same folly again.'

Why did he leave her with no argument, nothing to say? A sob caught in her throat and as he heard it his arms tightened cruelly.

'I've had just about all I can take, girl, for one day. Don't push your luck too far, or worry too much about being in my debt. Your tears will only enrage me at this stage. I should advise you to keep them for later!'

His words ringing, another threat in her ears, Ross subsided, thinking it almost funny that they should be quarrelling so sharply while so close to each other. He asked her to be quiet, yet his nearness, acting as it did like an intolerable stimulant, would not allow her to relax. She tried to sleep again, but could not. In the end she rested silently against him, her eyes closed but every nerve on edge, until they reached the oasis.

Hours later she was conscious of being lifted from the horse's back and that Armel ben Yussef was carrying her into her tent. There were many excited, chattering voices, and she thought she heard Jamila's among them, but suddenly not able to face them, she kept her cheek turned against Armel's broad chest, pretending she didn't hear.

With relief she heard him dismissing them all curtly, and the tent flap dropping behind him. He carried her swiftly through to the inner room, laying her on the bed. Her eyes fluttered open and she managed to look at him. She felt so stiff and sore and miserable it was a real effort, but she did not want him to think she pretended to be asleep. He knew well, because she had kept gazing at him during their long journey, that she was not.

'If you can manage to undress,' he frowned, staring down at her disreputable trousers, her torn shirt, 'I'll bring you a drink. Then I shall collect my own things and sleep in the outer tent, so as to be near if you need me.'

Ross woke the next morning with the same sense of fear she had known after Armel had rescued her the first time, and again she felt exhausted, scarcely able to move. Whatever he had given her had certainly removed the persistent ache from her limbs, but she still felt weary. As if since yesterday she had lived through a hundred experiences and come through none of them very well.

So much for the success of her little ventures! Bitterly Ross reflected. Did disaster have to follow her wherever she went? Never, she vowed, would she try anything out of the ordinary again. There were Freddy and the boys who might have done better without her, even if none of that episode had been exactly her fault. If she had not allowed herself to be persuaded in the first place none of that might have happened. As to this second, equally infamous event—well, there could never be any doubt that she had been entirely to blame for this. Overcome by remorse at the thought of her poor horse, Ross buried her fair head in her pillow and began to weep. Salem, for all his wickedness, she felt too ashamed to think about.

Without warning the flap of her room opened and Armel walked in. She knew who it was right away because she recognised his firm tread. Or was it simply that her senses were coming instinctively to know when he was around? He seemed to move like a tiger in the night. Probably because of his devious career he had trained himself to approach on quiet, cat-like feet.

He spoke softly too, if there was still a thread of steel in his lowered voice. Twice he murmured her name and, when she made no immediate reply as she was trying desperately to stem her regrettable flow of tears, he put a hand on her hunched shoulder and far from gently turned her round.

Staring down at her, he regarded her tumbled hair, the tears streaming wildly down pale cheeks. 'Aren't you feeling any better?' he asked, so coolly that, in spite of realising what she owed him, she felt infinitely worse.

She could only look at him helplessly, her blue eyes filling unconsciously with a nervous apprehension at the sight of his hard self-assurance. 'I don't know why I'm crying,' she confessed, on a far from elegant little sniff. 'I can't seem to stop. I expect it's just reaction.'

He merely nodded as he picked up her wrist, frowning at the suddenly accelerated pulse rate. Ross, terrified that he should guess it was because he had touched her, let him assume she was frightened that he might punish her for what she had done. Her faltering speech to this effect obviously did not impress him.

'Like all women you are not prepared to pay for your crimes,' he taunted, his face hardening. 'This time I think you have been punished enough, but if there is to be a next time, be warned! I will not show you the same leniency twice. I will personally see that you suffer.'

Ross lowered her fair head again, his coldness drying her tears as nothing else could. Furtively she rubbed the last of them away, childishly, with the back of her hand. She deserved what he said, but the implications of it made her shiver. 'I suppose you are barely civilised,' she mumbled recklessly.

'That you might well find out,' he retorted laconically enough, but she could feel his gaze stabbing her downbent head.

It was like a fight, a battle all the way, and he didn't believe in sparing her. Why did she have to feel so hopelessly drawn to a man who could only hurt her? Yet his attraction was such that she had to steel herself against him, to strive to be cool and detached when she secretly only wanted to be in his arms.

'Aren't you going off on your travels again?' she inquired impulsively, trying to isolate such an alarming thought. 'My behaviour yesterday must have ruined your chances of—er—doing what you set out to do.' She hesitated to mention outright his questionable career—the spoils he might have gathered if he had not come to her rescue.

A slight smile quirked his wide lips as if he understood quite well what she had tactfully not referred to, but he merely said, 'No, Rosalind, I am not going anywhere. Not until you are ready to come with me.'

It was obvious he didn't trust her any more. 'What about your men?'

'My men don't expect to travel today.' His glittering eyes taunted her. 'They know I have my woman to see to.'

'Your woman?' she gasped.

'That is how they regard you.' His gaze rested with interest on the colour that came and went hotly in her pale cheeks. 'Ill-gotten gain doesn't come into it. They consider I came by you honourably.'

So he was back at that again! It was just as probable he had no business to take him away. He would never, she felt sure, stay here specially because of her, but had he any idea, when he talked like this, what he did to her? He wore his white headdress this morning, bound around with the usual rope cords, but his burnous was missing and his light shirt was open to the waist. He was handsome and arrogant enough to take any girl's eye, but he had something beyond mere good looks which would bind a woman to him irrevocably.

Feeling a whole lot like a fly caught in a web, Ross tried desperately to fight such an attraction. 'There were men with you when you first found me. They must know quite well the true facts.'

His dark brows rose mockingly. 'So?'

'Well,' she floundered, 'in the circumstances, if they have the wrong impression, isn't it up to you to tell them the truth?'

He said, very soberly indeed, 'The truth, Miss Lindsay, is something you're often wary of speaking yourself, but should you concentrate on it a little it might surprise you. Any day now you're going to have to come to terms with yourself and you will find that nothing but your heart has anything to do with the final reckoning. As for my men, it is better they believe you belong to me, otherwise they might be tempted to take the same liberties as did Salem.'

A pulse beat heavily against the white skin of her throat. She did not follow everything he said, but his words tormented her curiously. 'Salem was my fault, I told you.'

'He had taken to following you around.'

'How did you know that?'

'I know everything that goes on here. Unfortunately, in this case, I didn't learn quick enough. I was only given this information, along with two very interesting sheets of paper, this morning.'

'Oh,' Ross couldn't prevent the guilty flush, nor wonder at his sardonic tones.

'You're quite an artist, *mademoiselle*. In fact it is obvious you have much natural talent. Your sketch, which must undoubtedly have been executed in haste, I find incredible.'

Distrusting his compliment, she mumbled ungraciously, 'I've done a lot.'

'No doubt. What I am more curious to learn is how you managed to get hold of the necessary material. You asked Jamila?'

'No, she knew nothing,' Ross confessed.

'You went to my tent?' he drawled.

It was more of a statement than a question and she knew it would be little use prevaricating. Armel had a knack of discovering that which she would rather he didn't know. She realised she had trespassed and that he waited for an apology, but if she had to do penance for everything he considered a crime she would never be off her knees. 'Yes,' she muttered defiantly, refusing to look at him.

'And did you discover nothing else besides two pieces of paper on your small tour of exploration?' he asked cynically.

Beneath his wary gaze she felt herself go tense. 'I didn't explore, if that's what you mean. I merely took what I went for and ran.'

Strangely enough this seemed almost to satisfy him. As he stood contemplating her thoughtfully, she rushed on, saying impulsively what she hadn't meant to a moment ago. 'I'm sorry, Armel, but I couldn't think of another way to make Salem understand. I didn't know where else to go. But you can see now that your other men can be told the truth. I promise not to approach any of them again.'

His dark eyes never left her but gave nothing away. 'I spent the night in this tent, girl, in the other room. How do I explain that?'

Ross felt startled surprise go right through her and something else she could not name. Nervously unsure, she bit her lip. 'You did?'

He nodded with a kind of grim humour. 'I told you I was going to before you went to sleep.'

'And,' she gulped, 'what did I say?'

'You didn't say anything, but when I mentioned it you visibly relaxed. I took your approval for granted.'

'Probably it was because of what I had been through. I think I was still afraid.'

'Perhaps of the wrong man, *mademoiselle*.' He shrugged, his eyes on the pure curve of her throat. 'Once you screamed out and I came and held you in my arms until you slept again.'

Her blue eyes dilated as they were drawn helplessly to his. She tried to remember, but could not. A fire began to throb through her veins, the same subtle excitement she had known before. He had held her and it seemed suddenly a deprivation that she hadn't known. It could never happen again. Despair tore through her and it didn't seem to matter that his eyes told her quite plainly he was aware of all she was thinking. Finding some sense, she murmured at last, her fair head drooping, 'I couldn't have known.'

'Maybe not, but you put your own arms around me and begged me not to let you go. Almost I didn't, *mademoiselle*.

Having you close to me like that is not something I could endure twice and keep a cool head. You melted against me, Rosalind, and clung.'

'I must have been delirious!'

'But it still leaves you breathless?' Armel regarded her parted lips coolly. 'No, *chérie*, I chose to think it was more than delirium, but I will leave you to work it out for yourself.'

Suddenly, for no reason other than to escape the tumult inside her, the feelings she must endeavour to hide from him, she cried wildly, 'I ran away! Doesn't that speak for itself?'

His glance taunted her again. 'And I was almost believing you wanted to stay! To share a tent forever with a rough desert man.'

'You know that wouldn't be possible!'

'I know it is said that anything is possible if one wants something enough. Now, I should advise you to rest.'

Ross gazed after him as the tent flap closed behind him and she felt tears come again into her eyes. If only he had been a rough desert man—but she knew instinctively he would never be that.

To her surprise, during the following days Ross saw quite a lot of Armel. She had not thought he was serious when he had talked of not going away again until she was ready to go with him, but when he began to teach her to ride properly she began to suspect he meant what he had said. After the first week he took her daily on short excursions into the desert and when they went alone Ross treasured these outings against the time when she would only have memories to ease the loneliness of her heart.

It was on these excursions that he talked to her about the desert, the Moroccan people, their way of life, their Moslem religion. Once he told her that throughout the Koran, which is the Islam equivalent of the Christian New Testament and about the same length, the emphasis is laid on charity and justice. Above all it taught that Allah is a forgiver. The good Moslem prayed five times a day and fasted during the month of Ramadan. Armel could explain such things so clearly that

Ross often marvelled, never having even the slightest difficulty in understanding what he tried to tell her.

He talked of other things, too. Of how progress, and in
some cases the lack of it, had affected them. He could go
back for centuries, quoting reams from history, to the time
when Morocco became independent in March 1956 and
Mohammed V took the style of King until he died in 1961
and his son Hassan II succeeded.

Morocco, Armel said, had been through difficult times,
with many adjustments to be made since independence, but
in his opinion, had done remarkably well.

Ross could not pretend not to be interested, and listened
eagerly, but it was the people rather than history which
interested her most. This was probably a thing she had in-
herited from her father and she regretted, as she had done
often, not being able to speak of him to Armel. He already
knew of Ross's growing affection for the camp children, a
love which they undoubtedly returned, but he occasionally
laughed, to her utter mortification, when he came across her
attempting to cook. He would stand, tall and dark in his
snowy white burnous, and her heart would begin to race
uncomfortably. He would grin tolerantly at her amateurish
efforts to follow the Arabic instructions of the women
around her, and offer sober if not very helpful advice. She
couldn't seem to get the flavour exactly right, but sometimes,
when he condescended to taste what she was trying to make,
he pronounced it not too bad.

When he was amused and forgot to be stern like this Ross
felt an almost irresistible desire to respond. It actually hurt
that she had to keep such a careful watch over her impulsive
emotions, but since the episode with Salem the whole camp
seemed to look upon her exclusively as Armel's woman, and
the shyly knowing smiles of the other women often made
her go pink with embarrassment. Nor did it help that Armel
seemed never to notice the speculative glances they were
wont to cast over her slim figure, although he must have
been quite aware of what was so obviously in their minds.

As well as these other pursuits he liked to spend an hour
each day over her French. He made her read from one of the

few French novels he had in his tent and corrected her pro-
nounciation as she went along. Her French, he teased, was
atrocious, but after the first few days he told her she had a
natural ability and was doing well.

'In a little while, if you maintain the same standard, you
will be very proficient, Rosalind.'

While his praise pleased her she could not help wondering
why he did not consider Arabic to be more important, but
for some reason he refused to teach her this, although it was
something she suspected he could have done fairly easily—if
he chose. All she knew was the few words she had picked up
around the camp and from Jamila.

When one day she asked him about it again, he merely
shrugged and replied, 'French you will find useful wherever
you go, but you may never wish to return to Morocco.'

'Well, it's not so very important, is it?' If he could hurt
then she could try to, although she doubted she would ever
have the power to do this to him. That he could so easily
wound her she kept to herself. He was lordly enough without adding to his arrogance. To know that he could not
really contemplate keeping her here for ever should be
enough.

Strangely, as the days slipped past, Ross found herself
thinking hardly at all of life beyond the oasis. She was wise
enough to suspect that if Freddy had really tried to find her
he could have done—that was if he was actually free to do
so. Armel had said he was, and somehow, while she assured
herself she had no reason to take Armel's word, about this
she felt instinctively she could trust him. If Freddy had still
been in the hands of the desert nomad, she knew Armel
would have told her. Sparing her pain was not something
Armel indulged in; he could, when he liked, be quite ruthless and cruel, for all his more tolerant attitude towards her
generally. What frightened Ross now more than Freddy's
apparent desertion was the way in which her mind seemed to
be closing completely against the outside world.

Cousin Cynthia was fast fading, like an unpleasant dream,
with Armel ben Yussef becoming the dominating factor in
her life as the desert exercised its old inscrutable charm over

her. She did not want to leave. There was a warmth about these people she knew she would miss. Generously they had taken her to their hearts as if, without having to be told, they knew she had been starved of any real affection. Their way of life, Ross was aware, many would find primitive, but to her its very simplicity was indescribably beautiful—as was indeed the whole of that rugged country. The bare landscape no longer filled her with apprehension, the limitless miles of sand had long since ceased to seem empty. Now they provided innumerable subjects for her clever fingers to sketch, and the air was so clear she often wished for an easel and brushes so that she might paint the wonderfully vivid colours. Armel had given her a supply of paper and charcoal, but so far, apart from his first, he had made no comment.

But it was the moonlight over the desert which Ross had come to love most, when the oasis and sands were drenched in the palely glowing light and the silence was so deep that even a small sound like a heartbeat was magnified out of all proportion. When she walked with Armel on such magic evenings she often felt they were the only two people in the world, and that everything else ceased to matter. Not even his arms and his hard, bruising kisses which taunted and never satisfied seemed able to spoil the illusion.

Apart from the French lessons, which were strictly by invitation, she never went to his tent, although she occasionally felt curious about the many long hours he spent there himself. Each evening he dined with her in her own quarters, but never again did he sleep in the outer room. About an hour after dinner he would leave her. Then Ross would get to her feet and wander over the thickly woven rugs which covered the floor, her body possessed of a great longing she could put no name to. It was at these times she was forced to think again about escaping, before she lost control and could not subdue her tumultuous feelings. The future without him stretched bleakly enough without the possible humiliation of that.

So fearful was she of the future that when Jamila came to tell her, one afternoon, of some visitors who had arrived she could only stare at her in blank dismay. The first thought to

come to her head was that it was Freddy at last, but instead
of pleasure she felt nothing but dread. She would have to go
with him. There was no excuse to linger at the oasis any
longer. Armel might have recently paid her a great deal of
attention, but the feeling that smouldered between them was
probably only in her imagination. He had threatened, but
apart from sticking to his refusal to help her get away, he
appeared to have forgotten everything else. There was just
his mocking goodnight salute, otherwise he never touched
her.

That Jamila was disappointed because Ross made no immediate reply was easy to see. 'They are a troupe of dancers,
mademoiselle,' she went on eagerly. 'Berber dancers, who
will stay until tomorrow and have agreed to entertain us
tonight. Already we are preparing a feast. Sidi Armel has
graciously given his permission and there will be much to
enjoy.'

'A dancing team?' Ross felt her legs so suddenly weak she
was forced to sit down. So this was the cause of the girl's
excitement! 'I'm sorry, Jamila,' she smiled, 'I didn't understand. I thought . . .'

She broke off, biting her lip warily, not wishing Armel to
hear of her dismay when she had thought it might be her
half-brother.

But she had reckoned without Jamila's sharp wits. 'You
thought it was someone coming to fetch you away?' she
queried, her smile widening at Ross's white cheeks.

'It could have been,' Ross, to her despair, heard herself
floundering nervously.

'And you don't wish to leave—er—us?' Jamila laughed,
adding the last word so obviously that Ross was left in no
doubt that she had really been going to say Sidi Armel.

'Yes,' Ross spoke swiftly herself. 'That is—I mean, I will
be very sorry to leave you, as you must know, but neither do
I wish to outstay my welcome.'

'Of course not, *mademoiselle*,' Jamila agreed, keeping her
eyes, in which glinted a little mischief, downcast.

'The dancers?' Ross again spoke quickly. 'You seem very
excited about them. Are they so good?'

'Oh, yes,' instantly diverted, Jamila enthused. 'They are not just any team, *mademoiselle*. They do much, what is it you call it, professional dancing, but always they love to return to the oasis.'

'The oasis?'

'Any oasis, *mademoiselle*, when they tire of the big city, the oases and the great *kasbahs* of the north and south. There they will stay for days, dancing and feasting. There is much happiness and making love.'

In spite of herself Ross felt her cheeks grow hot. These people had a conviction that one was bound irrevocably with the other. There was nothing sordid or suggestive about their simple beliefs. It was a basic need, like music in their blood, which sought only the simplicity of outward expression. They had a very natural dignity, but would never understand the Western tendency to hide emotions behind an artificially indifferent front. When they wanted to cry they did, and when they felt like dancing and making love they did just that, with all the natural upretentiousness that mny other people had almost forgotten. Nor did the outcome of such normal reactions appear to worry them unduly. It might not always be wise, but another addition to a family seemed never to be stinted of love, whatever else it might be deprived of.

She was not sure about Armel's own views. He had, more than once, spoken derisively of her inhibitions, but then hadn't he referred to her supposedly loose behaviour with an equal amount of scorn? Uncertainly Ross clenched her clammy hands together. Would any girl ever know where she stood with a man like that?

Yet it was this very mystery of the East, this insidious enticement of the senses, that proved to Ross she must be wary. 'I will stay in my tent, of course,' she said at last. 'Apart from anything else it would perhaps be wiser. Better that no one should know I am here.'

Jamila, in the throes of going through Ross's wardrobe, turned with an anxious frown. 'But Sidi Armel sent me specially to tell you to be ready. I am to help you. He will be far from pleased if you do not come.'

Ross, too, frowned. Jamila's French, like her own, seemed to improve daily, although Ross suspected it had been quite good all along. Jamila chatted away, just so long as she wasn't asked too many questions, when she was apt to shut up like a clam. 'You haven't misunderstood? You are sure he wants me?' she asked hesitantly.

'I am very sure of that!' Jamila smiled, but a second later, when Ross glanced sharply at her sober face, she could find nothing to endorse the impression that Jamila's sentence could, quite easily, contain another meaning!

CHAPTER SEVEN

LATER, after Ross had rested, Jamila returned and helped her to dress. For a while Ross had continued to protest against Jamila assisting her in this way, as it wasn't a habit she wanted to cultivate. Cousin Cynthia would probably laugh at the very idea of it and accuse Ross scornfully of giving herself airs. Apart from this Ross considered herself too practical to need such help from anyone. She did sometimes wistfully admit to herself that it could be oddly comforting to be fussed over and spoilt a little.

This evening she wore a jellaba of thin white silk, and a sleeveless tunic, woven with a gold thread. She was used to such outfits by now and found them comfortable, yet she often felt they were too seductive and occasionally longed for the cool formality of a simple dress. Jamila brushed her long fair hair until it shone and streamed like a cloud of moonbeams over her shoulders. Ross, nervous in case it made her appear too abandoned, asked Jamila to catch it at her nape with a silver bow. She had no make-up, nor did her flawless, petal-soft skin seem to need any, but for once she allowed Jamila to apply a very little of the various powders and dyes she used. It couldn't, Ross thought, do any harm, and might give her some badly needed self-confidence as well as pleasing Jamila. She was surprised that the result pleased her too. The girl was really quite clever in the way she accentuated the lovely blue colour of Ross's eyes and smoothed a little clear pink into her fine, pale cheekbones.

It was growing dark before Jamila was quite satisfied with her handiwork and she led Ross to the other side of the oasis.

Ross could see, immediately they approached the leaping fires, that this must indeed be a festive occasion and that the members of the dancing troupe were honoured guests. Armel might be using their presence as an excuse to give his people a party but, whatever the reason, the visitors were being accorded true Moroccan hospitality. Many campfires burnt brightly where there was usually just one, and people were gathered in small, gay groups around them. The air was redolent with the smell of good cooking which mingled strangely with the more exotic perfumes of the women. It was at the women that Ross looked first. Somehow she had expected them to be dressed in the flimsy garments she had seen in pictures of dancers of the East, but these women were clothed as circumspectly as herself, their caftans of various colours covering whatever they might be wearing underneath. Their only concession might have been in the numerous straps of fancy beads and bangles they wore, the jewelled ankle decorations which jingled enticingly each time they moved their feet.

Jamila took her straight to Armel's side, although Ross would rather have stayed on the edge of the crowd. Sitting next to him she felt the focus of all eyes, the many interested glances which were cast in her direction. Eventually, as she gathered more courage, she lifted her shining head and did a little gazing herself.

'That's better,' she heard Armel say lightly. 'For a moment I thought it was going to prove too much.'

Ross started. He had been engaged in conversation with his head man and she had thought he had not noticed her arrival. Now, he took hold of her arm and introduced her smilingly to several of the visitors as a friend from England who was touring the desert with her brother. It surprised Ross that no one appeared to wonder where this brother was, or to doubt he wasn't around somewhere. Bitterly she queried why Armel had chosen to mention Freddy at all. It couldn't be that he sought to provide a note of respectability. He wouldn't care what construction anyone put on their relationship! It must simply be that he did not intend these people to imagine she needed rescuing.

People did not, she realised, question Sidi Armel ben Yussef's motives at all. He was arrogant and proud and when he gave orders he expected to be obeyed. When he made a statement he had to be believed. How did he do it? Ross could have said scornfully by the sheer weight of his dominant personality, but she knew it was more than that.

Not at all satisfied with her rather negative conclusions, she glanced again around the attractive faces of the women. Was one of them perhaps Armel's special friend? Some of them were beautiful with their golden skins and slender, seductive bodies and dark, melting eyes. They seemed to know him well, and the man who appeared to be their leader seemed very eager to talk to him. By the tone of Armel's voice and the interest in his eyes, Ross guessed he was asking the man a number of questions and, not for the first time, she regretted her inability to understand Arabic.

'Why don't you speak French?' she asked Armel crossly in English, when at last he turned away.

'Ismail is happier with Arabic,' Armel said briefly, gazing narrowly down at her, 'and he, too, is a guest.'

Ross flushed, not appreciating a snub he made little attempt to cover up. 'I'm sorry,' she rejoined coolly, 'I didn't realise. Jamila said they had just stopped by, so to speak.'

His slight smile still rebuked her. 'Don't you ever have unexpected visitors to your home, *mademoiselle*? Don't you make them as welcome as those you formally invite?'

Unhappily Ross glanced away from him. He wouldn't know she had had little recent experience of this. When her parents had been alive she could remember faintly how they had entertained a lot. Since then she had lost touch with that kind of family life. But in criticising Armel's manner with his friends she had been impertinent, and her heart sank as she realised he might justifiably be annoyed with her all evening.

'I'm sorry,' she murmured, her voice husky.

Armel sighed, his hand suddenly hard on her bare, slender wrist. 'I shouldn't have reminded you of your home. Now you begin to think of the quickest way to get there, but I should advise you to put it from your mind as such thoughts of it will not remain there much longer. Come, you must enjoy this evening, when I intend to show you what real hospitality is like. You look lovely enough to charm a thousand guests, *ma chère*, as well as myself. And I, *chérie*, intend to enjoy myself too.'

Ross's throat tightened at his words, and her pulse jerked as his lean fingers caught her wrist with an even greater pressure. If his tone had not been so threatening, her senses might not have churned so madly and she might have thought of something brighter to say. 'Did these people come on camels?' she whispered, trembling, not really curious.

Amusement quirked his firm lips, even while his eyes smouldered over her, regardless of the interested glances cast in their direction. 'No,' he answered, solemnly enough, 'They have horses. Occasionally, away from the desert, they have their own vehicles. Camels, you see, are not used nearly so generally as they used to be in these districts. But the Sahara, Rosalind, is still the largest desert on earth, with an area of some three million square miles, and there are places where the camel is still perhaps the most practical type of transport as they can go a long time without water.'

'I see ...'

'No, you don't. Nor will you until you have lived here for some years. One day, if you are really interested, I might take you deep into the Sahara. It isn't all a desert of sand, you know. But come, this is neither the time or place to explain such things. If you don't have something to eat, long before the evening is over you will be feeling faint.'

Ross was never to forget that night. The food was simple but more varied than usual. After the *harira* there was chicken and pigeons, prepared in different ways with saffron and honey and butter. There was mutton and rice, spiced to a delectable flavour by the cook's imagination. There were enormous, stuffed flaky pastries, baked by throwing small pellets of dough on the large metal griddles until the whole was covered with a thin film of crust. After it was baked it was removed and stuffed with whatever one chose. With all this they drank rosé wines from the vineyards south of Casablanca and afterwards ate the small, sugared almond cakes and drank refreshing mint tea.

Such a feast, Ross considered, was almost enough, but the dancing that followed proved an even greater treat. She had sat beside Armel during the whole of the lengthy meal, and while to begin with she had tried to stay distantly reserved it had been a poise she found impossible to maintain. When the dancing began she stared entranced, and as it went on the trembling excitement inside her was reflected in her bright eyes, the sparkling eagerness of her expression.

'You like it?' Armel asked, in a low voice, leaning nearer, his breath warm on her smooth cheeks. 'You have no difficulty in forgetting yourself for once.'

Without realising what she was doing, Ross moved closer to him while barely hearing what he was saying. She felt, rather than heard, his approval, being so absorbed in the performance of the players she paid little attention to his actual words. The Berbers' instruments might appear slightly primitive, but the music produced by the reed flutes, the tambourines, the skin drums seemed remarkably realistic and alive. They began with the *ahidou*, which Armel told her was a typical dance of the Middle Atlas region, in which men and women both participate. Ross watched as they stood shoulder to shoulder in a circle, clapping their hands and stamping their feet rhythmically. One man seemed to be leading the dance, conducting the melody and giving it its general direction.

After this Ismail sang. 'It is called the *quasida*.' Armel whispered, his shoulder touching hers. 'It will remind you of your English ballad and maybe make you sad. You are being reminded of your home too often this evening, are you not?' To make sure she didn't concentrate too closely, or so it seemed to Ross, he again took hold of her arm, the pressure of his fingers just enough to distract her attention. When the next dance, the *ahouach*, began, the fire was refuelled and the flames threw up gigantic shadows against the night. The whole scene seemed to be brought vividly alive as the surrounding desert echoed with the high-pitched chanting. This time the women danced while the men were the musicians.

There was only one solo performance, by a woman who seemed to have rhythm in her very bones. She even took

Armel's attention. Ross was very aware that he stared at this lone dancer until the dance was finished. She was strangely fascinated herself by the sinuous contortions of the girl's lissom body, but, woman-like, she saw no reason why he should be. Ross couldn't have explained herself why, after this, she stopped fretting against the restriction of Armel's hand and was content to rest lightly against him in the darkness until it was all over.

It was long past midnight before the campfires burnt low and he suggested she returned to her tent. The dancing and festivities had drawn to a harmonious close and people were drifting slowly away. In a few hours it would be dawn, the beginning of another day, and the dancing teams had a long journey in front of them. Armel's own people would also be up early to make them coffee and some simple meal for them before they set out.

'I don't feel terribly sleepy,' Ross protested, as Armel led her away. 'I could have watched longer.'

'A little of that goes a long way,' he murmured enigmatically, 'if one isn't used to it. It can be like strong drink.'

'I think you liked one of the dancers especially,' she couldn't help retorting, resentful that he appeared to think she was not mature enough to watch the more sophisticated dances.

Through the darkness she caught the glint of his white, self-satisfied panther smile. 'Could it be, my little flower of the desert, you are jealous?'

Ross wanted to deny this fiercely, yet before she was able to he went on, as if his remark could not really be questioned. 'I have long appreciated Yasmin's skill. Her talent is rare and inimitable. But then you, my small, enraged prisoner, have your own attractions. You have no need to envy anyone.'

Oddly disturbed, Ross would like to have declared she was neither jealous nor enraged, yet not sure she could do this with absolute truth, she retreated into a dignified silence. But her heart jerked when he called her his prisoner and she did not feel nearly so calm and collected underneath.

'You did appear to like our visitors,' Armel commented as

he strolled by her side, and her silence lengthened.

'They seem very nice,' she answered, adding primly, 'I liked the dancing, but otherwise how can I say? I had no chance to form a real opinion, seeing that you never let me get very near them.'

'I thought you would agree it was wiser you kept your distance.'

'If you should happen to be referring to my reputation, *monsieur*, I can't really believe you can be concerned. Not when you keep me here!'

'The women would not have insulted you with curious questions, if that is what you are thinking,' he said shortly, 'but it is better that they leave with the impression that you and your brother are simply two young people who have lost their way. This is not so unusual in the wilder parts of the desert to which you have rather foolishly strayed.'

Ross might have acknowledged the sense of this if she had not felt so strung up. Apart from anything else there was Freddy's own position to be considered. If he was in trouble, as Armel had hinted he could be, with the authorities, even by inadvertently crossing a frontier without the necessary authorisation, then the less attention drawn to him the better, she supposed.

'You think of everything,' she said bitterly.

'I try to,' he retorted calmly, 'and I should advise you not to worry. There will be enough opportunity to get to know the people, if you so wish.'

If she wished! Uncertainly Ross's feet stumbled on the fine sand and the soft south wind blew gently on her face. Sometimes she wondered how much longer she would have any will left of her own to make demands of any kind. She should be begging Armel to let her go with the dancers, but somehow she could not force such a request past her reluctant lips. Yet if she did not say anything wouldn't he immediately reach the conclusions she ought to avoid? 'Don't you believe it would be wiser if I went with them in the morning?' she whispered at last, her eyes, shadowed in the moonlight, fixed on some point far beyond his head.

Smiling slightly, he lifted the flap of her tent, thrusting

her none too gently inside. 'When a girl asks a man for advice it usually means she will be willing to follow it. It also points to some indecision. You are not sure? You long to stay, but you feel you must fight the dictates of your too impulsive heart?'

Ross trembled as she turned away from his dangerous astuteness. Fervently, as her pulse suddenly raced, she wished he would go. It had been foolish enough to walk back with him through the silent darkness, but the tent confined them too intimately. She had learnt, however, on previous occasions, that he would not go until he was ready. He was not a man to be ordered by a mere girl! Even so, she must make some sort of stand. 'My heart,' she told him defiantly, 'would never be allowed to dictate to me. I have too much common sense!'

Armel laughed outright as he caught her back against him before she had gone more than two steps. 'If you can rely on common sense, *ma chère*, after the wine we have drunk, the dancing we have seen, then you must indeed be a very cool creature.'

And clearly he wasn't convinced of it! Desperately nervous of her own similar doubts, she attempted to assure him, 'But I am, I always have been, and I can't think why you are here with me when more than one charming girl among your visitors seemed much attracted to you!'

Armel's air of amusement deepened as his eyes mocked her. 'I don't deny,' he said shamelessly, 'that there are times when I enjoy a woman's company, especially when I know my feelings are reciprocated. But you, my little moonbeam, my witch with the silvery hair, you really interest me! You resist me as if I were the devil himself, yet with others, with even less creditable qualities, you have not hesitated to respond very freely.'

Angrily Ross·gasped, as he derided her openly. She hated him when he mixed amusement with cynicism and cared nothing for her feelings. He drew her closer and she seemed powerless to stop him. She wanted to turn and run but she was rooted to where she stood. Around them the night closed silently, and it was still warm in the tent and his arm was like a band of steel around the narrowness of her waist.

'Please,' she whispered, 'let me go. Don't touch me!'

But his hand was already at her nape, with a quick twist removing the bow that confined her hair, brushing it back from her face when it fell like a thick curtain about her slender shoulders. Then his fingers were under her averted chin, his eyes calculating on her soft mouth. 'Don't you think you owe me a few kisses, girl?' he murmured, as she resisted him apprehensively.

Slowly he lowered his dark head, as if he realised she could not stop him taking what he so derisively asked for. With all her heart she wished she could, for he talked as if he were purchasing some trinkets in a market place. Trinkets he considered cheap!

'You know I can't stop you,' she said huskily, feeling her lips moving against his as she spoke, as his mouth caressed hers lightly before travelling gently to her ear.

'How badly do you want to stop me?' he whispered, his hands hard against the buttons of her caftan, undoing them deftly. He was expert at many things, she was discovering.

Helplessly her head moved as his breath came warm on her cheek, releasing something primitive inside her until, of their own accord, her lips searched yearningly for his.

His laughter had gone now, there was only a strange glitter in his eyes. 'Your hair is like a golden cloud with the sun shining through it, your eyes like the sapphires owned by the Queens of Ancient Egypt. Don't you wish to know how they loved, little one?' He held her to him, his words acting like a powerful drug as her caftan slid to the floor. 'You're like a small, lovely statue, *chérie*, a sleeping beauty waiting to be brought alive. What couldn't I teach you!'

'Armel,' she whispered, as his words went exquisitely through her, like pain. 'Please,' she entreated, 'you shouldn't say such things.'

He kissed her then, again lightly, his mouth tormenting, 'Why not, *ma chère*? Don't you care to know what I am thinking? Your own thoughts might interest me greatly.'

Her heart was beating so hard against him that she couldn't have said anything logical even had she tried. Even her lashes felt heavy, only seeking to rest on her flushed cheeks.

'So,' he drawled, 'you are unable to speak. You can only tremble in my arms, yet you declare you don't like me?'

'I'm not used to someone—to anyone like you,' she stammered, his mockery extracting a response while she scarcely realised what she was saying.

His voice was perfectly hard. 'You mean you have only known boys, like those you were with when I found you? It is a long time since I was a boy, *ma chère*, but let us see how you will manage a man. A girl like you has need of one.'

The ruthless smile was back on his face again, and before she could protest his hold tightened and he took her mouth almost before he had finished speaking, sweeping her close into the cruel hardness of his embrace. Her skin burned like fire, the sweep of it going right through her as his lips crushed down into hers. With a faint moan her slight body collapsed against him and, almost before it had started, his battle seemed won.

His white burnous joined her caftan on the floor as he picked her up and without taking his mouth from hers he strode with her through into the inner room.

Ross felt the softness of her bed beneath her and his strong limbs entangled in her own, but suddenly, as he aroused her expertly to ecstasy, she knew faintly that she didn't care. His lips were no longer cruel but unbelievably gentle as he pushed her thin silken tunic aside and explored her trembling body.

Her fingers touched his shoulders, then went around his powerful neck and clung as his passion began rapidly to consume her. She heard herself moan again and whisper his name, not once but several times as a wave of longing caught her and she melted into his embrace.

His hands went over her, their gentleness becoming something else again as he heard her entreating him not to let her go, and if he realised she didn't quite know what she was saying he gave no indication. She could hardly breathe, was unable to think for herself as she obeyed his every command. She seemed only to be swept towards inevitable surrender as they exchanged kiss for kiss, touch for touch, and he whispered tender endearments against her parted lips and soft neck.

Her senses reeling, Ross's fingers curled tensely into the hard muscles of his shoulders as he lay over her. Never had she known anything like this existed. Drawn almost to insensibility by the hardness of his utterly masculine body, she only strove unconsciously to get closer. 'I will stay with you, darling,' she whispered wildly, 'I won't ever leave you.'

'You would belong to me?' he muttered, his mouth taking hers passionately. 'You would be willing to spend the rest of your life here—with a desert man who scarcely has a penny?'

'I don't care,' she rejoined fiercely, her smooth young arms clinging to him. 'I wouldn't care what you had, or who you are!'

For a long moment he was suddenly very still, as if something in what she said had pricked him like a sword. He still held her, but Ross felt his instant aversion, and while she still—shamelessly, she realised—tried to hold him, it was as if he had withdrawn mental miles from her. There came a kind of ruthless coldness to him which she viewed frantically.

'Little brat!' he ejaculated curtly, pulling her arms from about his neck, throwing her almost cruelly away from him. His face contemptuous he looked at her, 'So I was right about you after all!'

Stricken almost to shock, Ross drew herself stumbling to her feet, her hands helplessly groping to cover her semi-nakedness as she did so. There was nothing here she understood, unless it was the shame which was swiftly replacing the passion that had nearly overtaken her. 'You know that's not true,' she said, staring at him dully.

'I know now it is.'

Suddenly, as she stood swaying before him, a sense of outrage stiffened her, saving her, as it did, from the utter humiliation of going down on her knees. 'You beast!' she cried widly. 'All right, I didn't behave discreetly, but I couldn't help myself. I know I should be ashamed, but I'm not! I've never felt like this in my life, nor been in such—in such a situation before. I know you don't believe me, but you can take that look from off your face! You knew what you were doing. I don't know what you had in mind, but now you can find an even greater satisfaction in laughing at me. And believe if you like that I'm no better than I should be!'

'Are you?'

'Oh!' Ross's face was white and mere words could never ease the churning fury inside her. It had to be something more physical. As if on reflex her hand flew out, making swift contact with his hatefully leering face.

Without uttering a word himself he lifted his own hand and slapped her back, his temper, on this occasion, rising as swiftly as her own. 'Now,' he snapped coldly, 'try to convince me you are any better than an alley-cat. You certainly are no more reticent. Like all women you're only too ready to rake over a man's past, to assume he has one, and you would run like the devil if you found it wasn't to your liking!'

Biting back a sob with the greatest difficulty, Ross stared at him, a tremor going visibly through her as she recalled how she had clung to him. Bred into him was obviously every restrictive influence of the East. He came from ancestors who only approved of women kept in the absolute seclusion of the harem. He pretended to be emancipated, but, when put to the test, he scornfully rejected it. He was convinced no decent Moroccan woman would have conducted herself as she had done.

Her cheek stinging, but not nearly so painful as her thoughts, she cried, 'You are obsessed with the past—mine, I mean. You force me to be indiscreet, then hate me for it! Well, you will find I can hate as thoroughly as you!' Her mind rebelled against such outright fiction, and it was a lie, so far as Armel was concerned, but she refused to be ground beneath his lordly heel, prideless into the dust.

His eyes narrowed, the glittering, mocking coldness deepening as they rested on the spreading red marks on her cheek. 'Maybe the next few days will prove the exact state of your emotions, girl, but I do not intend to be slapped each time you lose your regrettable temper. Until you learn to conduct yourself more modestly I should advise you to keep to your tent.'

Ross didn't see the sunshine against the side of her tent next morning. Everything about her ached, including her eyes which she rightly supposed were sore from crying. They had not been easy tears she had wept, but once started she had not seemed able to stop the painful flow of them, and they had done nothing to ease the hard restriction around her heart.

Now, as Jamila stood over her, softly calling her name, she buried her head deeper into her pillow, not willing that the girl should see her face which must surely bear too many traces of her last stormy quarrel with Armel. 'Don't worry, Jamila,' she muttered faintly, 'I'll get up later. I'd just like to be left alone.'

'Yes, *mademoiselle*,' Jamila's voice was still soft but a little firmer, 'I would do as you ask, but I'm afraid you must get up at once. Sidi Armel has visitors.'

'But they are going away!'

'There are others!' Jamila was clearly excited. Even without looking at her, Ross sensed it.

'Others?' she almost moaned aloud. She didn't even feel like facing herself this morning, let alone more visitors. 'How on earth have they managed to arrive so early?' she mumbled sullenly. 'Why didn't they come last night, as they must have been very near?'

Jamila's next words shook her. 'It is almost midday, *mademoiselle*. Sidi Armel said not to disturb you as you were tired. These people are his people and have been travelling since dawn.'

'His people!' Dismay sweeping through her, Ross jerked upright, forgetting her dishevelled appearance. She had not thought of Armel as having anyone of his own at all. 'You mean those of his particular tribe?' she asked, bewildered.

If she had been puzzled before she was even more so when Jamila smiled mysteriously. 'Sidi Armel belongs to none of our tribes, *mademoiselle*,' she said quietly, her eyes suddenly curious on Ross's tear-streaked face.

'And you can't explain? Or, more likely, you've been ordered not to!' Ross's voice was a mixture of weary indignation.

Jamila composed herself with dignity. 'My master will tell you all you wish to know, I am sure. He merely said I was to help you dress for a journey.'

'A journey?' As her pulse missed a beat, Ross felt herself go taut. By some devious twist of fate, in spite of what Jamila had told her, could it possibly be Freddy? When Armel had announced the arrival of their first visitors she had secretly hoped it would not be Freddy. To her terrible shame she had not wanted to leave Armel. This time she hoped fervently it was Freddy at last. After last night she only wanted to escape from Armel as soon as possible! 'Could it be my brother?' she breathed.

'No,' her spirits sank as Jamila shook her dark head, 'it is not he, that I do know.'

Sighing softly, she turned to search for something practical for Ross to travel in, and Ross knew that further questions would be futile. She would get nothing more out of her.

It was scarcely her fault, Ross decided, a little later, that she could do nothing much about her appearance. Her eyes, though not swollen, looked heavy and her skin was so pale that against it her mouth seemed both bruised and red. Jamila had found her a thick white burnous to go over the top of the thin cotton trousers which were the best they could find. Ross longed for a pair of serviceable jeans, but her only ones had been torn beyond mending. Ready at last, she drew a quick breath and, after thanking Jamila quietly for all she had done, walked out into the sunshine.

Feeling oddly shaken at the thought of yet another step into the unknown, Ross halted a short way from her tent hoping for a few moments alone to compose herself. But this, it seemed, was not to be granted.

Seeing her stop, Armel ben Yussef left the man with whom he was talking and strode swiftly towards her, the sight of him, so tall and proud in his flowing burnous, as always affecting her disconcertingly.

'You are ready?' His level glance went over her and she was left in no doubt he referred to her dress, not her inclinations.

He stood close to her and owing to a distracted trembling in her limbs it took a great effort to lift her chin, but manage it she did even if she could not quite meet his eyes. 'Your message seemed to leave me no choice.'

'Did Jamila say anything?' His voice was curt.

'If you mean did she tell me anything, then the answer is no, *monsieur*. She is too well trained—too afraid of you, I expect, to disobey orders. She merely said something about your people coming to see you, and that I was to prepare myself for a journey.'

'That was all?'

'More or less.'

He took no notice of the sudden despair at the back of Ross's clouded blue eyes. 'I am not going to enlighten you immediately, *mademoiselle*, but you had better know that my cousin has come seeking me. His mother, my aunt, is ill and has need of me. You will accompany us without delay.'

'Your cousin?' Forgetting her own unhappiness in the face of his bad news, Ross gazed at him anxiously. 'I hope your aunt is not too seriously ill, Armel?'

'I hope not,' he replied smoothly, as if acknowledging the inquiry of a distant acquaintance.

On a wave of bitterness Ross swallowed, exclaiming irrationally, 'I never thought of you having a cousin—or an aunt!'

His lips stretched ironically, 'My cousin is the son of Caid Ahmed el Alim. His name is Moulay and he is used to a certain amount of adulation.'

Startled, Ross's eyes widened with apprehension. How wrong she had been about Armel! She had thought of him as a wanderer, belonging to nothing or no one, a nomad living off his wits. And hadn't she been prepared to share that life with him without reserve, last night! Only she had never been given the chance, and now she knew at least one of the reasons why. He was related, by the sound of it, to some of the highest in the land. How he must have laughed at her while she had clung to him, laced her arms around his neck and almost begged him to take her. Her cheeks were already scarlet with mortification when she heard him add:

'My cousin has a regrettable weakness for attractive young women. I must warn you not to be too responsive.'

'You're detestable!' She could actually feel the heat in her face.

'You didn't think so when I held you, just a few hours ago!'

His expression made her drop her eyes in confusion as she recalled his hard searching hands, his sensuous mouth. 'No gentleman,' she cried wildly, 'would ever refer to such a thing—nor blame the innocent party!'

His eyes continued to mock her. 'No innocent would have behaved as you did in my arms. Your nails left some very interesting marks on my shoulders, and not because you were trying to get free.' His glance smouldered with a narrowed satisfaction, a hint of threat. 'You escaped lightly last night, girl, but do not try me too far. There are plans for my cousin which do not include girls like you, and I do not intend my aunt should be further upset. In fact, should you give any trouble I will take steps to see no one is left in any doubt as to whom you belong.'

Ross's throat was too tight to allow her to reply. There was only her whitening face to express her feverish shock.

Armel went on coolly, not obviously bothered too much over her anguished silence. 'About the manner in which you arrived here—I have told Moulay much the same story as I related to our friends last night. I have merely added a few brief details as to how I found you. There is no need to elaborate. You will simply agree that you were not well enough, after your short skirmish with the nomads, to go on with your brother, and it was wiser to rest here until he returned. Such an explanation is quite feasible and respectable, you will find. If you act with some circumspection people will accept it without question. Otherwise, I'm afraid, I can't help you further.'

'Armel . . . !' In suddenly overwhelming despair his name seemed drawn from her lips, but whatever she had been

going to say was frozen at birth by the coldness of the look
he slung at her as, grasping her arm, he drew her ruthlessly
over the sand to meet his cousin.

Moulay el Alim, when Armel introduced them, stared at
Ross with undisguised admiration. He did not resemble
Armel greatly and she felt a sense of relief. Moulay was
darker. Whereas Armel's face was tanned to a smooth hard
brown, his was definitely swarthy, and his eyes were black.
Yet they were both tall and broad and from a distance, Ross
thought, one might easily be mistaken for the other.

Moulay bowed low over her hand, lifting it to his lips to
kiss it lightly. Obviously practised in the art of pleasing a
woman, he did nothing to frighten her. 'So this is why you
choose to linger long in the desert, cousin?' he teased Armel.
'Who could blame you!'

He spoke so charmingly, and in her own language, that
Ross found she could take no offence. Indeed the warmth of
his eyes was so comforting after Armel's harsh handling of
her torn emotions that she could not resist the temptation to
ignore the censure in Armel's face and smile back at Moulay
warmly. 'I owe Sidi Armel a lot, *monsieur*,' she flushed, 'but
I can assure you he does not linger in the desert because of
me.'

'Sidi Armel!' Moulay's teeth gleamed white, with more
than a flicker of amusement.

Ross's long lashes flickered uncertainly. 'I am very sorry
you bring bad news of your mother,' she said hastily as
Armel stood grimly not speaking, leaving her to flounder.
As an apparent stranger her position might make such a
query too pertinent, but she had no means of knowing.

Moulay did not seem to think so, however. It seemed the
sort of politely solicitous remark he expected. He continued
to smile on her approvingly. 'My lady mother is sometimes
foolish, I'm afraid, and while as soon as the good physician's
back is turned she forgets to carry out his orders, immediately she feels ill again she shouts for him!'

And everyone else, apparently, Ross thought, wondering
what manner of woman this aunt of Armel's was. Unless, of
course, she was seriously ill and wished to have her family

around her. Aware of Armel's darkening expression, she felt a little ashamed of her uncharitable conclusions and asked quickly, 'How long will it take to reach your father's home, Sidi Moulay?'

'Several days, I'm afraid. His *kasbah* is deep in the desert, and, as you must know, our desert is not like your Hampstead Heath.'

'With luck we might shorten this time,' Armel suggested, before adding on a note of growing impatience, 'if we leave right away. If not, then you could add another week.'

Decisively ignoring her, he set about giving orders to this effect, leaving Ross gazing after him, the hurt in her eyes causing those of the man who stood watching her to narrow speculatively over her young, transparent face.

CHAPTER EIGHT

Ross was surprised to find they were to travel by camel. Noting Moulay's expensive apparel, the impression he somehow gave of unlimited affluence, she had expected Land-Rovers, even a helicopter. But Armel, when she had the opportunity of asking him about it, merely laughed.

'One can't do exactly as one feels inclined. As I've told you before, we have frontiers. Apart from these the Sahara is very difficult terrain. Being so vulnerable to strong winds it is constantly changing. Overnight the wind can whip up mountains of sand a thousand feet high and veritable craters in ground which on the previous day might have been perfectly level. Even Land-Rovers with sand wheels still have their limitations under these conditions, and horses, too, have obvious drawbacks.'

'But you use horses yourself,' she pointed out.

'Yes, because they are ideal for my purpose.'

Ross thought it might have been nice to have known what his purpose was, but knew better than to ask. Up on her camel she felt rather like a boat on a rolling sea, if she did soon get the hang of it. If it hadn't been so hot she might even have enjoyed the experience. Perched, as she was, about seven feet from the ground, she had a much better view over everything than she had ever had before. Armel rode by her side and his camel, although appearing a beast with a discontented nature, obviously knew better than to challenge the man on its back.

Ross, though grateful in a way for his close company, found it disturbing, especially each time he turned his haik-bound head to ask if she was all right and his eyes lingered for several intent seconds—probably, in spite of her determinedly airy reply, to see that she was in no danger of being a nuisance by falling flat on her face, Ross decided bitterly, not enjoying the curling sensation inside her each time she met his considering glance.

They rode on through the heat of the day, when the sun was so fierce it reduced the power of thought to the absolute minimum. The motion of the camel, which Ross eventually got used to, made her feel slightly sick. This, combined with the heat, brought on a kind of stupor that caused her to be more aware of bodily discomforts than those of the mind. For a while she half closed her eyes, giving in to the lassitude rather than fighting it, until slowly it began to leave her.

When she had first travelled the desert with Freddy and his friends, from the back of their truck, the never ending sand had seemed only monotonous. Now Ross found she was discovering a beauty in it that she had not previously noticed. The simple, uncluttered lines had a purity, a wonderful clarity of colour that she guessed would never be found elsewhere. Many places in the world might be beautiful in the usual accepted way, but none could be as breathtaking as this.

From the pommel of her camel saddle, under the immensity of the desert sky, the bare rocks and flowing sands formed landscapes of stark but wonderful simplicity. A silent emptiness, strikingly beautiful, space which seemed to stretch interminably to the needle-etched line of the horizon. There were mirages in every direction with the clear water of tree-lined oasis pools floating with tantalising inducement whichever way Ross looked. A large tree offering much-longed-for shade changed into one of short stunted growth as they drew nearer, and a huge rock, offering much the same facilities, she was puzzled to find was only a small stone.

While the pure white light of noon seemed to strip away every vestige of colour, the softer shadows of approaching evening provided relief from the harshness of the day. It brought new depth to the blueness of the sky and the vast, yellow sands. As the sun went down the horizon turned to purple and red, with clouds gathering low against the skyline. Thrilled, Ross pointed these out to Armel, but he said they were too thin to provide rain, if this was what she hoped for.

Ross, who could at that moment think of nothing nicer, merely shook her head.

By the time they made camp beside a small oasis, the moon had risen. Swiftly, by its light, a fire was built and two tents were pitched a short distance away. One, Ross was grateful to be told, was hers. As the other was only large enough to accommodate one, she wondered whether it was Armel or Moulay who chose to sleep out beneath the stars. Moulay had with him what appeared to be a small army of men, one of whom proved quite a remarkable cook. While the fare was not so varied as that of Armel's camp, it was substantial and good. Afterwards she felt tired but content.

Soon after they had arrived she had been brought a pitcher of water. There was not a lot, but it had been enough to allow her to wash away the dust and sand. Much refreshed, she had dried herself quickly, regretting that she had no change of clothes. It made her realise, not for the first time, how desperate was her situation, and she resolved to speak to Armel about it if she got a chance. It was no joke to be lost in the middle of the Sahara without a penny to her name. She would have to borrow, find some means of getting home as after they reached Caid el Alim's *kasbah*, Armel would no doubt be too occupied with his own affairs to give hers another thought.

As she did not want to think of the time when she would not see Armel again, she had hastily dealt with her hair and left the tent. Her hair had gleamed like liquid gold in the moonlight and she had felt the eyes of many of the men resting on it as she had eaten. Moulay had seemed absorbed, and startled by its pale beauty even though she had knotted it discreetly at the back of her head. He had not seen it before as for her journey she had worn a thick veil.

'A madonna,' he had said, disregarding Armel's cold stare, holding her hand much longer than was necessary after he had guided her to her place for supper. 'Such wonderful hair, Mademoiselle Lindsay, is enough in itself to

enchant a man. I could wish sincerely that Armel had not
found you first.'

Her face flushing deeply, she had not dared look in
Armel's direction. So sensitive was she to his every mood she
could almost feel his disapproval. Not even when he had
laughed carelessly and said, 'You'd better remember that,
cousin!' had she been able to do more than stare down at the
plate of food before her and tremble.

She was trembling slightly now as she approached him.
The camp was quiet, the men having retired some distance
away and Moulay having gone with one of them to inspect a
camel. Rather nervously Ross came to where he lounged
contemplatively in the shadows, and asked him about
Freddy.

'I know you won't want to listen, but he really won't
know where to find me,' she muttered, imagining a little
belligerence might impress him more than tears.

He turned to her savagely, his eyes questioning her wavering defences without pity. 'Do you actually wish him to find
you, Rosalind? You seem too intent on enjoying yourself in
the desert.'

'I don't know what you mean.'

'I do have eyes,' he snarled. 'I warned you about Moulay.
Why in God's name did you smile at him when he mentioned your hair? He's impressionable!'

'So you told me.' Ross was bewildered, defensive, running
a gamut of emotions. 'More than you are—I realise,' she
cried bitterly.

'I'm more than ten years older. He is barely twenty-six.'

Recklessly, because his unfair suspicions hurt, she exclaimed, 'Many men in my country are married long before
this age, *monsieur*!'

'And girls of your age too,' he agreed suavely. 'How is it
you have escaped this questionable fate, Miss Lindsay? With
your particularly loving nature . . .'

'I've never met a man I've wanted to marry!' she interrupted, trying to insert this small piece of information
sharply but only succeeding in choking. 'There are other

things in life besides the acquiring of a husband,' she finished sullenly.

'Perhaps you're too choosy,' he mocked, 'or is it your boyfriends who are?'

Her lips quivered as his taunting tones seemed to bring actual pain, but she refused to give him the satisfaction of knowing how much he could wound her. For a long moment he regarded the pale, stubborn face before him, then said heavily, but with quiet emphasis, 'Moulay's bride has already been chosen. She happens to be a girl from a family with a good measure of royal blood in their veins, as has Moulay's. It would prove a great blow to his parents if anyone was to upset these plans at this stage, and I should hate to feel even indirectly responsible.'

'Responsible?' Ross could not bring herself to believe what it seemed he was trying to tell her. She must have the wrong impression.

'By bringing you along when I should have left you in camp. By being over-concerned that you might come to some harm should your brother's reprehensible friends find you again. For putting temptation in Moulay's way.'

Did it really matter how much more he flung at her? The agony that was tearing her apart could not be worse. 'I don't know why you should be so apprehensive about me,' she whispered, her pulse racing at the dark condemnation she could detect in his face through the grey moonlight. 'I think you exaggerate greatly. Moulay has only known me a few hours!'

'And I hear how already you are so easily using his name, while not even yet, after so many weeks, can you bring yourself to speak mine naturally. And haven't I seen how he looks at you for much longer than necessary, as if he would like above all things to know you better!'

'You're mistaken . . .' Because she could barely control it, her voice rose in wild denial.

Like a tiger he pounced, grasping her wrist to tumble her ruthlessly down beside him on the sand. He was suddenly too near as he rasped, 'I do not allow hysterics, girl. Last night your kisses were like honey, your body like a flower coming to bloom in my arms, waiting for the rain to fill its opening petals with rapture. You knew exactly how to make a man want with every sinew of his being to make love to you. And now you dare to tell me you don't know what I am talking about!'

Ross's face felt the heat of his furious words and she trembled, the flame from her imprisoned wrist searing through her, ruthlessly indifferent to her slender fragility. She had not known a man could be as cruel as this. 'I never asked you to kiss me,' she gasped.

'You didn't want it?'

Helplessly her bright head went down at that. In that moment to deny the truth seemed almost to deny her whole being—which was something beyond her present experience. 'Yes,' she whispered, 'I did.'

His dark eyes continued to rake her unmercifully, not content that he could reduce her to such a state of non-evasion. Her odd trembling seemed merely to amuse him as his lips curled. 'So, *mademoiselle*, I should advise you to seek your bed, and a little honest contemplation. I shall be sleeping just outside, should you imagine you have a scorpion under your mattress and be tempted to shout for Moulay. I will warn you once more not to linger in his company or I will not be answerable for the consequences!'

Though abject misery struck her dumb, Ross felt her temper rise beneath the weight of insults he poured on her hapless head. 'I will smile at whom I like, and you can't stop me from being pleasant to your cousin. Or any man,' she added defiantly but unwisely.

Armel smiled coldly, twisting her treacherously towards him, his grasp so tight she was held immobile. 'If it's a man you want, you will have to content yourself with me,' he said savagely.

Before she could move he caught her swiftly to him, lowering his mouth to part her shaking lips with unnerving ferocity. 'Put your arms around me, girl,' he muttered, 'and kiss me properly. I don't want a naïve little girl.'

His steely voice, wrapped in velvet, commanded softly

and, unable to resist the now familiar flare of melting feeling, Ross found herself obeying like someone without a will of her own as her body slid helplessly to his. The ringing in her ears became intolerable, his hard hands and mouth pain, until as suddenly as it had happened the previous evening, she found herself thrust away. As she almost fell from him she glimpsed at Moulay's tall figure pausing abruptly before turning from them and she was aghast to imagine what he must have seen. Armel, she had little doubt, had planned this final humiliation on purpose.

'You really are a devil!' she cried, stumbling to her feet, her hair tumbling past her shoulders, flying in wild disorder as she left him and almost ran to her tent.

For nearly a week they travelled in much the same manner as they had done on the first day. Ross, although she would have died rather than complain, often found it very difficult to keep up. In many ways she grew tougher, but the heat of the sun, together with the remorseless pace Armel set, would have exhausted a far more acclimatised traveller. She had soon mastered the art of camel riding, although the actual mounting of the animal still filled her with apprehension. It crouched to allow her to mount and, as it straightened its legs, the jolt always threatened to impale her on the pommel of her saddle. Once comfortably seated, with her feet bare against the camel's neck, she didn't feel so bad. It wasn't this which occasionally made her feel ill. It was the whole weight of her many worries, not least her love for Armel which seemed to be growing in intensity in spite of herself. That he had taken very little notice of her since the first regrettable night beside the oasis, when he had threatened all sorts of things, she accepted as logical, if with pain. But the despair that swept over her whenever she glanced at him riding beside her was sometimes almost past bearing. Her appetite slowly disappeared and she grew thin.

Each night, keeping his rather dubious promise, he slept only a few yards from her tent. In other circumstances she might have derived some comfort from knowing he was so near, but it only seemed to add to her heartache to hear him tossing in his sleeping-bag, as if he slumbered no more than she did.

She could not seem to fight his hard dictatorship, and heaven knows she tried to. He drove them all relentlessly, not sparing anyone, least of all himself. It did not help that even Moulay's men appeared to like and respect him and obeyed without query his every word.

For Moulay's benefit, Ross supposed, Armel pretended to be more attentive than he actually was. He never left her side for long. What Moulay made of it was not clear, but there had been times when she had caught him staring, almost wistfully, as if he would have liked to know her better, if he had been given the opportunity.

If Ross found consolation in anything during these peculiarly timeless days, it was strangely enough the desert itself. It became a kind of love-hate relationship which she had never experienced before, unless it was with Armel. Certainly no place had ever drawn her so tenaciously and, while she did not admire everything about it, she marvelled at its many moods. When the wind rose and the sand began to blow, as happened frequently, she felt its vicious hostility towards her and all living creatures. It was these minor sand storms she came to dread most. The blowing sand and dust could reduce visibility to nil, while at the same time intensifying the sun's glare, and she would find herself crouched over her pommel, the leading rein in Armel's hands, almost praying that the wind might drop, or that she might die an easier, more comfortable death.

But once, after rain, she had been thrilled to see how the same desert had almost flowered. The rain, which had fallen overnight, had nearly scared her by its very intensity, and when she rose the next morning the whole desert had a very different appearance.

Armel, to her surprise, had aroused her in the half-light of the early dawn. She had looked up to find him crouched over her, his hand insistent on her bare shoulder.

'Get up,' he had whispered swiftly, 'I tried shouting, but you were dead to the world. I've something to show you.'

She had sat up with a startled jerk, and hours later she

could still feel the impact of his eyes going slowly over her.
To her dismay, instead of being immediately conscious of
what he said, her sleep-drugged gaze had sought his face.
The warmth and texture of his skin, the instant appeal of his
powerful, lean body was all she had been aware of.

'Armel!' she had whispered, and, as if unable to deny the
compulsive magnetism between them, he pulled her ruthlessly close, seeking her with both his hands and lips. It had
been a moment she could never forget, nor would want to
remember. In the early morning, her mind emptied of all
restrictive thought, it had seemed incredibly wonderful, if
dangerously stupid, to cling to the source of such miraculous
delight.

But Armel ben Yussef had been up an hour, and his mind,
as always, was alert and fully conscious. Brutally, he wrenched her clinging arms away. 'You don't have to act like a
little animal!' he'd exclaimed scathingly, turning derisively
from her. 'I'll give you five minutes. As you have nothing to
take off it shouldn't take you long to put something on.'

Almost she hadn't gone. It was only after she had acknowledged that there could always be such frightening moments
of awareness with Armel, and it was foolish to allow herself
to be so wounded by them, that she had found the strength
to get up. He might have his faults, but she realised he was
in many ways wiser than herself. If he hadn't gone, in
another minute it might have been too late. He liked to call
her naïve, but she had been instinctively aware of his passionate desire before he had cast her so forcibly aside. He
wanted her, but he would never give in to such weakness,
not with a girl he considered as inferior as herself!

Yet in the desert that morning his gentleness had been a
revelation. It might have been that her pale, cameo face,
etched with lines of tense exhaustion, had moved his conscience in spite of himself. He had been standing only a few
yards away when she had at last left the tent. Glancing at her
as she had come to him, his eyes had darkened to a sudden
intensity which had made her limbs tremble. But instead of
hauling her to him, as she felt he would like to have done,
he had taken her hand, leading her away from the camp, the

recumbent, still sleeping figures of men, and pointed to the sky.

Dawn, the first she had seen properly, had proved another revelation. Ross, her fingers curled submissively in Armel's, felt moved beyond words, as if she were seeing the beginning of the world, the heavens remade before her very eyes. There had been the deep violet blue of the night sky, against which the pure etched curve of a new moon still hung like a piece of palest gold. But instead if darkening, the horizon was now tinged with the most wonderful hues of gold and red. It was like the sunset but even more dramatic as, like a flame, the first rays of morning burst all around them and the fluffy cumulus clouds which had brought the overnight rain could be seen rapidly dispersing.

'The stars,' Ross whispered, 'will all be gone, too, in a moment.' Her voice was awed, low-toned with wonder.

By her side she had heard Armel laugh gently as he had carried her hand to his lips, 'The legends have it,' he'd murmured, softly, 'that the stars are no more than small holes in the tent the Gazelle threw over the earth in an attempt to trap her lover, who always left her before dawn to avoid revealing his ugliness.'

In a revealing flash Ross had wondered if he was referring obliquely to his own scarred hand and, instinctively, her eyes had left the panorama before her to flicker over it.

If he had noticed, his face had been inscrutable. Slowly he had released her and turned her away from him so that she might see that rarest of sights, the desert blooming. 'Look,' he had said, still softly.

Ross had looked, and been amazed. For days they had travelled, and, apart from the oases, she had scarcely seen a tree or even a few tufts of grass. Now, as the light grew stronger, she saw that patches of flowers suddenly carpeted the gravelled slopes which were appearing as they approached the mountains. Many of the sand dunes, too, had a covering of what seemed like grass, and there was another kind of green plant among their feet that Armel told her was a type of low spreading melon.

Further on he allowed her to kneel and examine some

yellow daisies, and there were some white and blue flowers
rather like the English crocus. The variety of colours was
surprising and occupied every hollow, every small puddle.

She was unaware that her companion gave more attention
to her animated face, noting her delighted absorption at each
new discovery, then her incredulous horror as they came
across the camels devouring great mouthfuls of the low-
growing vegetation.

'You must stop them!' she remembered crying rather
foolishly, but it had seemed sacrilege that they should be
allowed to destroy the beautiful, newly born flowers.

Armel had merely smiled tolerantly and asked who could
blame them. 'They enjoy a feast as well as anyone,' he had
said, 'and before nightfall the plants will normally be all
withered. Don't begrudge them a dewy bite while they can.'

While Ross had stared at them doubtfully, he had gone on
more dryly, 'Flowers are rather like a woman's emotions,
you know, girl. One imagines, seeing them in all their perfection, they are indestructible. It is a lesson to be learnt that
they do not always withstand a worsening change of climate.'

Recalling another time when he had hinted sarcastically at
the very same thing, the quick indignation Ross experienced
had dispelled her glowing appreciation of the morning.
Armel, also, seemed suddenly to find it not much to his
liking as he had taken her impatiently back to camp, where
he had instructed the now stirring men to see immediately to
the camels—but not because of her concern for the flowers,
she soon learned, but because of his haste to be gone.

As they approached Moulay's home two days later, Ross
realised she knew no more about Moulay or his family than
she had when they had started out. Once or twice, when she
had thought Armel to be in one of his softer moods, she had
tried to ask him for a few details, but he had always curtly
told her to wait and see. Now that they were just a few hours
away, she felt extremely nervous, not so much of what she
didn't know of his aunt, but rather of what his aunt might
discover about her. Of course if this aunt was very ill she
would not be up to asking questions or even seeing Ross at

all, but she might just as easily be recovered as it was many days since her son had left in search of Armel.

Ross stirred anxiously as she sat beside Armel in the leading Land-Rover, heading swiftly for the Middle Atlas. By comparison to her camel she supposed this must be the height of luxury, but the longing which occasionally overcame her to be back in the desert with Armel was so great that she often felt she would have done so without a flicker of regret if she had been given the opportunity—which of course she was not.

Once at the Caid's *kasbah*, she had little doubt that Armel's first intention would be to pack her off home. It was strange that she had heard nothing about Armel's own family when it seemed his must be as affluent as Moulay's. All the way here it had been he who had given the orders, Moulay who had obeyed.

Armel ben Yussef drove, she noted, as expertly as he did everything else, and no matter what he was doing he always looked annoyingly immaculate. Glancing at him sideways, Ross was made very aware of her own untidy appearance. She had had no change of clothing since they had left his camp at the oasis. Each evening, in the small allocation of water she had been given for washing, she had tried to rinse her undies. These had usually dried sufficiently for her to wear the next morning and at least were fresh, but her outer garments she felt frankly ashamed of. If she had looked better she might have had a little more confidence for the talk which she felt could no longer be put off. As it was she could only do her best.

'Will I have to meet your aunt?' she asked tentatively, her eyes slipping from his strong, forceful profile to where his lean hands with the two slightly misshapen fingers lay firmly on the steering wheel. They had left the camels at the edge of the desert where they had transferred to what had seemed to Ross's bemused eyes like a fleet of Land-Rovers.

'Naturally,' Armel answered her query absently, 'but this will depend on her state of health. It may be a while. However, you will need a few days to refresh yourself.'

'I will have to borrow some clothing again,' Ross muttered unhappily.

'This can easily be arranged,' he said smoothly, 'although I should have thought there should be more than sufficient in the pile you had at the oasis for your immediate needs.'

'I didn't bring them along,' she confessed slowly. 'I'm afraid I didn't think about it, perhaps because I didn't realise we'd be leaving in such a hurry.'

'I gave Jamila explicit instructions to get you ready.'

Did he have to talk as if she was a parcel, or an infant! 'It might have been my fault,' she hedged, seeking to protect Jamila from his possible wrath, 'I can't remember exactly what she said.'

His sigh of audible impatience was cut short by a quick frown. 'Then what the—what on earth have you been wearing?' he exclaimed, moderating his language with obvious difficulty.

'What I wore when I left.'

'You mean to say those are the same things!'

'Don't they look like them?' she cried sharply, a remark she regretted as soon as it was out, as his eyes came swiftly over her, noting how the thin, wind-torn garments clung to her gently perspiring body.

'It doesn't matter,' she added with more constraint, while thinking bleakly that he might realise now why she had slept with nothing on. 'I won't need a lot. Just something for possibly a day or two until I get back home.'

His frown deepened. 'I'll supply everything you want,' he said curtly, as if there could be no argument about it. 'And I will personally contact your parents.'

'My parents?' Ross's blue eyes flickered anxiously to his decisive face. She hadn't forgotten about this looming problem, but she had hoped to be in a position to make her own arrangements for getting back to England, without having to confess this last misdemeanour.

'Yes, your parents,' he repeated sardonically. 'You don't imagine they could be worried?'

'You don't have to put yourself to any more trouble.' She

tried to ignore his sarcasm as she brought her gaze back to her lap where her fingers twisted, full of nervous tension.

'Oh, it will be no trouble, I assure you!'

How she hated the suave tones, the underlying but unmistakable threat! 'I will be leaving for England almost immediately.'

'You think so?' His lips curled visibly.

'Wouldn't it be rather foolish if I didn't?' she retorted, striving for a firmness of voice. 'I mean, we do seem to be getting near to civilisation—and civilised behaviour. It would be stupid to pretend otherwise!'

His eyebrows rose. 'You have not seen my uncle's *kasbah*, Rosalind. It is almost as isolated as the desert we have just left. In places there are few tracks over the Atlas mountains and roads are non-existent in some areas. I will have no time to help you immediately, so you must be prepared to stay a little longer. I do promise, though, to contact your parents.'

Once more she tried, through the tumult inside her. 'It would be better if I rang myself. That is if you do have telephones at the *kasbah*?'

'You will leave them to me!' He did not answer her question directly. 'I am not yet willing to relinquish you, *mademoiselle*.'

Her heart jerking, Ross refused to ask why. But she now knew him well enough not to doubt what he said. It frightened her greatly, but the truth seemed no longer something it was possible to evade. Anyway, she thought, feeling suddenly inexplicably weary, what was the point? Armel's opinion of her, as he discovered how she had further deceived him, couldn't get much lower than it already seemed to be!

'I have no parents,' she said starkly, after the manner of one jumping in at the deep end, her eyes closed, her breath held.

The Land-Rover swerved, so roughly that Ross's eyes flew wide open again. Armel's swift glance through his rear mirror confirmed her suspicions that if the others had not followed so closely he would have pulled in and stopped. 'Would you mind repeating that, Miss Lindsay!'

Her breathing, in the face of such encouragement, became even more difficult. 'My parents are dead,' she muttered. Then, hoping to forestall further queries, 'I live with a sort of distant relative of my father's.'

The ensuing silence was fraught with a tension she could almost feel. Hypnotically she couldn't take her eyes from his whitening fingers on the wheel. He must be—he probably had a right to be, very angry. 'I'm sorry,' she whispered hopelessly, 'I only pretended I still had them because I thought they would be some kind of protection. I acted on impulse, but afterwards I found it impossible to tell you.'

'As if I were some sort of monster,' he exclaimed harshly. 'I wonder how many more damn lies there are yet to uncover?'

The angle of his jaw unnerved her as much as his cruel query hurt. 'The atmosphere was seldom very convivial, not for confessions, at least. You can't pretend you would have been interested in a detailed story of my life.'

'You're being deliberately evasive. A few straight facts would not have taken seconds.'

Her face went paler. 'You never told me anything of yourself. Your own life . . .'

'Mine is none of your business.'

Tears stung her eyes as pain stabbed harder. 'And it would be ridiculous to go on pretending that mine is any of yours!'

He ignored this, but his breathing roughened, 'Where does this—er—distant relation come in, *mademoiselle*?'

'I've told you, I live with her, work for her.'

'I see,' he nodded mockingly. 'And naturally, as in all good stories, she is a tyrant?'

Ross stared stolidly ahead, the tears thickening in her aching throat, refusing to answer the sneering note in his voice. He spoke so rapidly in French that she had some difficulty in following, but his general attitude left nothing to the imagination. She wished, suddenly fiercely, that he could have met Cynthia and seen for himself. Cynthia could be very charming when she chose, but her face had always had a hardness which didn't easily deceive.

Armel concentrated on a bad stretch of road. When he spoke again his voice had softened slightly. 'We'll accept that you lost your parents, but whatever this other relative's faults or failings, you can't but admit you could be causing her great distress by simply disappearing?'

'I realise,' Ross's voice was more choked than she knew and she made no attempt to deny what he said. That Cynthia's distress would be for her personally she very much doubted, but Freddy was another matter. He had always been the apple of her eye. 'She's bound to be alarmed,' she added vaguely, thinking aloud in terms of Freddy.

'So,' Armel agreed, severely, 'we must get in touch immediately.'

'No, please!' The cry rose to Ross's anguished lips as she thought of Cynthia's anger, the whiplash of her contempt. Involuntarily her hand went out to clutch his arm and the vehicle swerved dangerously.

With a half smothered curse he dragged it back on course. 'I'd advise you to control yourself, *mademoiselle*. My cousin will wonder what's going on! I simply intend speaking to your relative and to let her know you are safe and where you are staying. My uncle's credentials could not be faulted, child.'

'I could be home in a few hours, I'm sure, if you would help me?' she protested, her shaking hands now firmly clasped in her lap.

'You are in too great a hurry to leave me,' he drawled. 'I think a week or two here will be necessary, unfortunately. You need rest and building up, especially if all you have to return to is hard work. These last few days have been more of a strain than you realise. You are in no fit condition to travel any further—not right away.'

Ross's fingers curled. She had more sense than to translate his words into sympathy. Whatever his reason for wanting to keep her here it was certainly not that. Perhaps, like a jungle cat with a mouse, he liked someone to torment! Well, he would find such high-handed methods cut no ice with her. She would never be a willing victim. That she had no wish to have him speak to Cynthia did not mean she didn't want to return to England. After all, it was the only place she could go to, but she had made up her mind—and goodness knows she had spent long enough thinking it over, all those long, silent hours on that camel. She would write to Cynthia and tell her she would not be back to work for her again. Once Cynthia had got over the shock of having to replace her with paid labour she doubted if she, Ross, would receive another thought.

'I could always appeal to the Caid,' she retorted.

Armel's broad shoulders shrugged indifferently. 'My uncle is a very busy man, Rosalind. He is also an important one. You might have some difficulty in presenting your case in a way guaranteed to gain his sympathy. And don't forget you are my business, not his. He wouldn't thank you for asking him to interfere.'

'There is always your aunt,' Ross said, on a note of desperation. 'She is a woman.'

'Naturally.'

'You don't have to be so sarcastic!' Ross turned in her seat to look at him furiously. Her cheeks flamed as he momentarily removed his gaze from the road to meet her eyes coolly, hating him vehemently for making her love him when his only desire was so obviously to torment her. 'She is a woman,' she repeated stubbornly. 'She would listen.'

'No doubt she would, being notoriously kind-hearted, and normally curious. But rest assured, whatever her personal opinion she would not go past me either.'

'How nice for you,' Ross retorted, blinking back some bitter tears, 'to be surrounded by such loyalty. I'll find someone, someone somewhere, who will help me!'

He simply shook his head dryly, as if both her threats and herself were without substance. 'No, Rosalind. You will rest for a while as I seek to uncover any further deception. Then, when I have you straightened out, we will decide sensibly what is to become of you.'

CHAPTER NINE

THEY reached the *kasbah* of Rabouet late in the afternoon. After the flatness of the desert the stony approach to the mountains had confused Ross strangely, making her not altogether sure that she didn't prefer the burning yellow sands they had left behind them. Huddled in her seat she waited, the apprehension in her heart not soothed by Armel's unsympathetic silence, for what lay ahead.

The skyline lay long and straight, broken by the high, jutting peaks of rocky pinnacles and lonely plateaus where Ross would not have been surprised to see an eagle soaring. The country was wild, the sky high, the deep crevasses to the valleys intimidating. They followed a dry river bed at the bottom of a canyon and the road was rough and difficult, the whole length of it being strewn in places by small boulders which had fallen from the sheer cliffs above. The sandstone flamed, yellow and red, in places black and cruel-looking which chilled her more than the weird bright colours, which, if curiously macabre, were not so frightening.

Miles they appeared to travel through the various gorges until they eventually arrived at Rabouet. It stood on a kind of tree-dotted plateau, the mountains behind it providing a backdrop of unquestionable beauty. In order to reach the Caïd's residence they had to turn off the main track and, after the hills of arid-looking stone with no signs of vegetation, the vast oasis with its feathery palm trees was a welcome sight.

The Caïd's residence lay at the end of a tree-lined avenue, a combination of massive, tower-like blocks to a height of several stories. It sprawled, as if the builder had almost forgotten to stop, its white, crenellated ramparts looking as if they could defy the strongest army. As they swept through the entrance gate Ross was surprised by the grandeur of it all. It was, at first glance, completely overwhelming with its

large inner courtyards, its shady terraces and walled gardens
startling to Ross's eyes, so used had she become to the bar-
renness of the country outside. It looked more like a palace
than the house of even a rich man, and the bemused glance
she slid at Armel was oddly tinged with resentment. There
was even a little anger that he had brought her to a place like
this without even giving her any indication as to what to
expect.

In one of the inner courtyards the small convoy came to a
stop. Armel came around to her door immediately he eased
his tall frame to the ground. He did not help her out but
waited until she climbed stiffly down before taking her arm
in a firm, don't-try-to-escape-me grip. She walked like this,
between Armel and Moulay, into the *kasbah*.

Inside was a huge complex of chambers and galleries and a
coolness, which after the heat of the journey, Ross appreciated more than anything else. Yet it was all so opulent she
found it difficult to restrain her wandering eyes. In the
manner of a sleep-walker she took in the floors of fine
mosaics, the walls covered with tiles of intricate patterns or
carvings of arabesque. Silver lanterns were suspended from
the ceiling of the reception room where she stood and velvet-
covered sofas lined the walls. Rich silk-embroidered hassocks
of many colours lay on the beautiful rugs which were scattered over the floors, contrasting yet blending so wonderfully
as to be wholly pleasing to the eye.

Armel interrupted her rather dazed staring by jerking her
none too gently towards a man who came walking quickly to
them. It seemed he had been waiting. She was introduced to
his uncle, who looked not unlike an older edition of Moulay,
but had a kind of presence which reminded her more of the
man whose fingers still curved steel-like around her arm. For
a moment she felt an uncertain compulsion to bow. The
Caïd's own expression was kind but guarded as he greeted
what was an obviously unexpected visitor, as he listened
politely to Armel's brief explanation of how Ross had been
lost in the desert. He looked as if he was about to offer some
advice, but Armel gave him no chance.

'If Miss Lindsay could be given a room,' he suggested

smoothly, 'I am sure she would be very grateful. We have
been travelling a long time and I think she is weary. And I
would like to see my aunt...' He frowned, not attempting
to disguise a certain anxiousness, 'I hope she is no worse?'

'No, indeed!' the Caid smiled. 'She is, in fact, much
better, a surprising recovery. Perhaps we have been too hasty
in summoning you so impetuously from your desert, but you
will understand we were alarmed. As for a room for Miss
Lindsay, nothing could be simpler.'

The Caid, looking incredibly Westernised in his elegant
suit, seemed only too happy to oblige his arrogant nephew,
although Ross doubted if the allocation of a room for one
such as herself came anywhere near his sphere. He was
courteous and charming, and his air of efficient command
was no myth. Within minutes she found herself whisked
away by what she supposed was the Moroccan equivalent of
the English maid, up the sweeping staircase to the vast
portals beyond.

Armel made no attempt to follow. He only said not to
leave her room before he saw her again, which should be
very shortly. His tone was impersonal, his eyes so cool, there
was nothing to betray that they had ever been anything more
than strangers. Perhaps, because she must look such a posi-
tive tramp in her now soiled ragged clothing, it was the only
impression he wished to give.

Once in her room, Ross found she was so tired she didn't
greatly care. There must obviously be a set of rooms set
permanently aside for visitors as the maid stopped at the first
door along the wide, arched corridor and ushered Ross
politely through it. She thanked her and the girl smiled her
appreciation, the warm friendly smile of the East.

She ran a bath, a deep one, that made Ross feel immediately guilty, even while she stared at it longingly. Water was
in such short supply in the desert. While this was obviously
not the case here, she felt she could never use it casually
again. The girl could speak no English and her French was
not as good as Ross's had been before Armel's careful
tuition. In the end Ross gave up and decided recklessly to
take what the gods seemed very generously to offer. She

immersed herself almost lasciviously in the warm scented water and waved the girl away.

It was heavenly, after the deprivations of the past weeks, just to soak. She scrubbed every part of her with the scented soap, then washed her hair, which felt full of sand and dust. There were huge white towels to dry on, and, afterwards, she wrapped herself in one of these and lay on her bed. After sitting in the Land-Rover all day she might have been wiser to have tried a little exercise, but her body felt so bruised and tired after the punishment of the rough terrain over which they had travelled that she could manage no further than the large, silk-draped bed.

Here she slept deeply, scarcely being able to remember, when she awoke several hours later, ever reaching it. The maid was sitting by her bed when she opened her heavy eyes, but as soon as she saw Ross was awake she disappeared, so swiftly as to leave Ross thinking she must have imagined it. Gasping a little when she glanced at her watch, she struggled to her feet. She felt refreshed from her bath and sleep, but her hair, which she had only managed to rub half dry, was still damp, and a towel seemed all she possessed in the way of clothing.

Outside it was dark, she could see through the light drapes about the window. There was no moon, but the stars looked familiar, their brightness stirring memories she would rather be without. How had she ever managed to get herself into such a fix? On top of everything else it seemed a kind of ironic grand finale to have fallen asleep. Hadn't she planned to do such a lot before nightfall! Yet here she was, several wasted hours behind her and unable to do a thing about it. She could scarcely go careering around an Arabian Nights palace like this in a bath towel and, search as she might, her few scraps of clothing seemed to have gone.

Just as she was scuffing her bare toes uncertainly on the polished sheen of a priceless rug, the girl returned carrying a tray, followed closely by Armel. In startled surprise Ross stared, forgetting for a moment even her embarrassing state of undress. He had discarded his rough desert attire in favour of a white dinner jacket. In it he looked so disturbingly handsome it did things to her pulse.

'You've slept,' he said, after sweeping Ross coolly with his eyes and exchanging a few words in Arabic with the maid, who immediately put down the tray and left.

Ross nodded, her eyes still fixed tensely on his. 'I don't recall intending to,' she answered automatically, 'I only remember sitting on the edge of the bed. I can't really remember having a good look at my room. The bath was lovely, I enjoyed it. I washed my hair, but it hasn't properly dried. I think . . .'

'Rosalind,' he interposed rudely, 'will you kindly shut up! You're like a record player gone out of control.'

'Oh . . .' Ross wished for the thousandth time he couldn't so easily reduce her to about five years old. He probably thought of her as that age too, although a second later she changed her mind as he drew nearer and his gaze lingered on the bare curves of her body which the towel left exposed. 'I'm sorry,' she gulped, sitting abruptly down again and dragging the towel closer around her, 'I think I still feel a little dazed, and I can't seem to find anything else to wear.'

'I can't think of anything that might suit you better,' he offered smoothly, gallantly polite while his eyes still probed, arousing a most peculiar response inside her which she was thankful he could not know about.

'How is your aunt?' she asked hastily. 'I hope, as your uncle said, she really is better?'

'Much better, thank you.' Ross fancied he sounded a bit grim as he went to a small toilet table she hadn't yet noticed and picked up a comb which he silently passed her.

Her hair must have been responsible for the dry note of disapproval in his voice. Defensively she drew the small curved comb through her tangled, tumbled locks. 'I couldn't see one before,' she said righteously, 'and I've only just woke up. Besides, I'm not sure you should be here!'

'Don't worry. They know of your exhaustion.'

'You mean they know what you told them?'

'Yes.' The bed slumped as he sat down by her side.

'And they believed you!' She wished he hadn't chosen to sit just there. It was very difficult, well nigh impossible to comb one's hair satisfactorily while holding on to a towel!

'But of course. In a thing like this they would.' Calmly he took the towel from her clutching hand and held it himself. 'You can't do two jobs at once,' he observed, as if attuned to her thoughts, if not the degree of her agitation.

She could have been quicker if her hands hadn't trembled so much. Ruthlessly she tugged the comb, unaware of pain as his fingers grasped firmly but spread widely and were not still on the high, firm curves of her figure, she knew he must feel the frantic throb of her heart and was glad that the fluffy disorder of her newly washed hair hid the rather tortured expression on her face.

Her hair was done and she flung aside the comb as though it burnt her. He simply laughed, surrendering the towel again but grasping her bare shoulders, turning her to him slowly as he lowered his mouth to hers, playing with her lips gently but tantalisingly until she relaxed and responded, feeling her senses whirl as he pressed her closer.

Another minute and she was free. 'As I was saying,' he began conversationally, as if such an interlude had never happened, 'my aunt and uncle very rarely question my opinions.'

Ross started blindly to eat her supper, not really seeing it. 'You appear to be an acknowledged authority on many things, but I have yet to discover the exact nature of your— er—work!'

Again he laughed coolly. 'I shouldn't despair. I have little doubt before you are many days older you will have learnt much of what you so wish to know. Only I can not guarantee that any of it will please you.'

'But it has never been your intention that I should be pleased, has it, *monsieur*?' she gritted, trying desperately to subdue her body's unconscious dissatisfaction. 'You have always been intent only to punish.'

'And it had to be my own cousin who saved you from the fate I had planned so cruelly. You'll be telling me next you are pleased to have left the desert?'

The exact context of such diversity escaped her. 'No—I mean, I don't know.' How could he expect her to betray the fact that she had come to care for it—as she had him? She shivered still to recall those nights, the dark hours in his arms. Arms which had never meant to be kind but had been around her all the same. In this house Armel seemed to move in no recognisable sphere and so many things could come between them, circumstances which she felt almost tangibly even while, as yet, she knew nothing of them.

He was watching her taut face closely, as if he enjoyed all her patent uncertainty. 'You are not the only one to suffer regrets, *mademoiselle*, but we have not reached the end of the road yet. And while escape seems wholly to consume your mind, I have news which might persuade you to stay, no matter what I ask of you.'

News! Concerning herself? Shaken, Ross pushed her supper tray from her. Surely he hadn't managed to get in touch with Freddy already? Or home? That was it! Her eyes widened with the old familiar nervousness. 'Cynthia?' she whispered, her cheeks slowly paling of the last pink flushes of sleep.

'Yes,' he agreed, not smiling although there was a slight pleasure in his eyes, as if he enjoyed her too aparent apprehension. 'One would suspect, Rosalind, that you do not appreciate this mysterious relative?'

'I'm sorry,' Ross replied stiffly, making a great effort to pull herself together. 'Of course I owe her a lot . . .'

He smiled cynically, his gaze cooling. 'How often does one have proof that most things come easier than gratitude? That the debtor is always last to recognise the source of his benevolence!'

'Because one is often not allowed to forget such a debt and is expected to pay an exorbitant interest,' she choked, wondering why she allowed herself to be provoked. He had the power to hurt her and he used it deliberately, this she knew.

His eyes glinted. 'And you chose to concentrate on this rather than any sacrifice your guardian might have made?'

'If you like . . .' Ross felt suddenly too weary to argue further. Why didn't he just get on with it, instead of tormenting her as he was doing by asking questions she couldn't properly answer?

'You would consider anything you owed me in exactly the

same light?' His voice, cool and cutting, sliced through her thoughts.

'It didn't cost you all that much, did it!' she flared, driven painfully. 'I seem to have paid back quite a lot.'

He watched the fresh flame of colour with interest. 'You've given nothing voluntarily. Everything I've had I've had to extract with force. When you come to me openly, of your own accord, and acknowledge your debt against my lips, only then will I consider your obligations partly cancelled.'

She gripped her hands together tightly, not realising that the gesture was becoming too familiar, a sure indication of her inner tension. Trembling, she wrenched her clinging gaze from his. How could he talk so easily of such things? It was like a deliberate seduction without even touching, and Armel did it so naturally he might have been passing the time of day. Was this a rude reminder of the difference between East and West, a difference she had long since, it seemed, forgotten? 'Only partly cancelled, *monsieur*?' Was the answer so important as to make her forget the conversation he had just had with Cynthia?

'You have it right first time,' he assured her, smoothly arrogant. 'As for the rest, we shall see. Once you've got that far anything else will not prove too difficult. You can take my word for it.'

'As I will never get as far as that I don't need such assurance,' she gasped.

He merely smiled, apparently indifferent to the trouble she was having with her breathing. 'Unfortunately we must concentrate on the call I've just made. We might indeed be wiser to remove the obstacles one by one—and together. This way you will never feel you had no control over your own destiny.'

Ross waited, her mind, as if slightly bemused, swinging, exactly as he dictated, back to Cynthia. 'What did she say?'

'A lot I shan't repeat. After I had convinced her there was no possibility of my reversing the charges she quite let herself go.'

She ignored his sarcasm, taking no comfort from it. 'Does

she know where I am? What had she to say about Freddy?'

'I gathered he has told her almost everything. Or at least his side of the story,' Armel added smoothly.

Startled, Ross stared. 'Then he's been in touch with her? He's safe?'

'Better than that, *ma chère*, he is with her!' Armel's voice came dryly.

'Back home?'

'Yes, girl. Several days ago.'

Shock ran relentlessly all the way through her, bringing a cold perspiration to her pale brow. 'He must have given up trying to find me.'

'I'm still doing my best to work out how hard he tried. Judging from the length of time he's been home he didn't over-strain himself.'

There was nothing at the moment Ross could find to refute this, although she found it hard to believe that Freddy had simply gone off and left her with scarcely a backward glance! Unsteadily she asked, 'Why did he leave his two friends?'

'They probably left him,' Armel replied cynically, his eyes on Ross's knuckles which showed white against the white towel she still clutched to her breast. Her bare, slender shoulders drooped, but she did not seem aware of it. 'They didn't strike me as being the type to hang around with anyone liable to hold them up. Probably your disappearance bothered them. They might have imagined some trouble with the police, and, if their reputations are anything to go on, they certainly wouldn't want that.'

'I see—and so he went home.' Her voice came flatly, her face devoid of colour, reflecting her inner fears unconsciously. 'I've been all sorts of a fool, you don't need to tell me, but I thought ... Oh, never mind ...' With weary effort she tried to cast aside such useless regrets and form another query. 'Did either he or Cynthia say anything about my money, my return ticket, which was in my luggage?'

'No.'

'But Freddy must have known it was in the truck. How

does he expect I'm to get back?' Much as she tried to keep it
low her voice rose hysterically.

'Calm down, *chérie*!' As if he realised how near breaking
point she was, he spoke with cool authority. 'I assured your
guardian she could leave this to me, but I'm afraid I must tell
you she doesn't wish you to return. Not to her residence at
any rate.'

'But why?' Bitterly shaken, Ross added, 'She couldn't
deny I was extremely useful!'

'Apparently she has found someone else to take over your
duties, the daughter of some rich citizen who feels she must
justify her existence by finding a job. Freddy discovered her.
She appears, for various reasons, to suit them both.'

'And she has taken my job?'

'I'm afraid so, although you don't have to take my word
for it. She is very eager, this relative of yours, to speak to you
herself, just in case you don't get the right message, but I
should advise you to let her cool her heels for a few days.'

Numbly Ross lowered her fair head, missing the derision
which, this time, was not directed against herself. She
thought she knew of this girl Armel mentioned. She was the
only child of wealthy parents and Freddy had been angling
for an introduction for a long while. Cynthia, of course,
would welcome her if there was money. She had too much of
her own not to appreciate the worth of such a commodity. It
was unlikely there would ever be any place for Ross again.
Briefly she glanced at Armel again. 'What exactly did she
say?'

His mouth tightened. 'A very great deal. That she took
you from an orphanage, brought you up, that you'd always
been headstrong, difficult to handle. That you will no longer
be welcome in her home. There were so many faults I began
to doubt if they might ever be contained in one so slender
body!'

'I see.' Ross's small white teeth bit painfully on her full
lower lip, but she felt nothing, the hurt inside, which she
had thought she had long been immune to, returning to
torment her.

'Talk about it,' Armel commanded, instantly perceptive. 'How long were you in this orphanage?'

'Until I was seventeen.'

'From when?'

'From when my parents died, when I was ten.'

Armel frowned sharply, as if doing some quick calculations of his own. 'Why did you need to go there at all? Why did you not go immediately to this Cynthia?'

'Because she had a business to run. I expect because she was always so successful she had no time to spare . . .' Ross paused, then went on. As Armel seemed intent on uncovering everything she might as well tell him briefly what he wanted to know. There was nothing remarkable or even very unusual about her story. She made short work of it, finishing after a very few minutes. She gave only the bald facts, so numb that it no longer seemed important what he thought, yet unable to look at him when it was over to see a condemning expression.

'So,' he said eventually, breaking his curiously taut silence, 'you must now put all this behind you. There are certain matters, but as I have used almost all my present supply of restraint, I will not immediately pursue them. As a fully trained secretary, personal assistant and everything else, you will be invaluable here for the time being. After you have saved a little money from your earnings you may decide for yourself what you wish to do. I am sure you wouldn't wish for a loan that you perhaps could never pay back.'

Tears stung Ross's eyes. His sympathy was like a mirage; it never really existed. 'I shouldn't trouble you at all! I'm sure my half-brother will send me as much as I need, now that he knows where I am.'

'Then shall we say until this happens?'

'Just so long as you realise,' she whispered, still reluctant to believe Freddy would do nothing to help her. She blinked away her tears furtively before looking at Armel again. 'You sound very sure I will be accepted here.'

'Why not?' his broad, heavy shoulders lifted. 'My aunt is almost recovered, but must obviously cut down on her acticities. She has a great deal of correspondence over which she likes to keep busy. You will help her with this.'

'Will it be enough? I am used to long hours, *monsieur*, and dislike being idle, whatever your opinion of me.'

'You will rest first, you need it,' he rejoined sternly, unimpressed. 'If you find you still have time to spare I have a lot of work myself that needs expert attention. You can save me the bother of sending out for a secretary. Not many are so very willing to bury themselves out here.'

While she was pondering this Armel stood up, a quick lithe movement of his powerful body. 'I must go now, Rosalind,' his voice lightly mocked her mental turmoil. 'I think perhaps I have outstayed my welcome as it is.'

Ross said bitterly, 'I can't deny you've given me plenty to think about!'

His sensuous lips sneered, 'And you don't love me for it, eh, *ma chère*? Well, I should advise you to sleep again and not waste any more valuable hours fretting about your so solicitous relatives.'

All Ross could think about as he made sharply for the door was something to wear. 'My clothes?' she cried weakly, unable to envisage facing anyone else in a towel.

'Don't worry,' he paused briefly by the door, looking back. 'I will send your maid with some, and a more suitable robe. *Mon dieu, ma chère*,' he declared, with an ironic twist, 'if I must continue to supply you with so many clothes, you might well be my wife!'

Ross's breakfast was brought to her the next morning quite early, as if Armel had known she would be awake and hungry after failing to eat her supper. The maid also brought a selection of clothes, similar to those Ross had worn at the oasis. On her tray was a note containing a short message from Armel saying she was to stay in her room until he came for her.

Why did he insist she must not move without him? Unhappily Ross regarded her coffee and fresh, hot croissants with a diminishing appetite. She had a frightening feeling she was a prisoner again, for the third time since she had set foot in this country. She could almost have crept back to bed and wept, if her tears had not all been shed through the night into her pillow. While she resisted the temptation to do this, there was no evading the fact that each time she tried to escape she merely finished up in a worse position than before.

For a time, after she had toyed with her breakfast, she sat still, trying to think, then trying not to. Restlessly she choose a suitable caftan, wondering, as she had done previously, where it had come from. The size and colour was exactly right, it might have been made for her, moulding her figure as it did so closely. Suitably dressed, she now wondered where Armel had got to. Why, if she was to work for his aunt, was he not here explaining the precise nature of her duties? If his aunt was still ill, of course, she might not want her immediately, but he had said she could do something for him.

Yet, although she was curious about Armel ben Yussef's work, the thought of being with him daily seemed more than she could bear. What did she really know of him? If Moulay's marriage was already arranged, how about Armel? He was quite a lot older than Moulay. Wasn't it more than likely he, too, was committed, or had commitments somewhere which she knew nothing about? When his arms were around her she could convince herself she didn't care. He might, when the mood was on him, hurt her, but no other man had made her feel as he did. No other man was ever likely to while she loved him so desperately. Last night, when he had taunted her about being his wife, she had almost whispered how much she loved him. If he had shown the remotest signs of tenderness she had the most frightening suspicion that she mightn't have minded what he thought. It was only when she was away from him that she felt grateful for the cool streak of sanity she was still able to display, the cold light of reason that showed her clearly he was not for her.

Armel didn't arrive and Ross could easily believe he had forgotten about her. After months in the desert he no doubt had much to see to. The view from her window went over the gardens, the outer ramparts to the mountains beyond. She saw the road descending to the valley from the narrow,

lower plain on which the *kasbah* was built. The sun struck
rock and cliff to shades of pink, ivory and ochre, glancing off
the bare stunted cactus trees and hotly dispersing any furtive
shadow lingering beneath them. She had not realised the sun
could be so relentless until she had come here. Yet hadn't she
grown fond of it, learnt to enjoy its warmth while acknowledging its power, in this tropical land, to wither much of
what it touched? Only men who were equally powerful
could withstand it. Thinking at once of Armel, she shuddered.

Turning with a jerk from the window, as if burnt by even
the thought of him, she decided hastily that she could stay in
her room no longer. It was well past mid-morning, he
wouldn't come now. Cautiously she opened the door and
slipped out.

Armel had given her to understand, the evening before,
that she had been put near the family quarters as there was
no other guest staying at present. There was no one around
but not wishing to disturb anyone she went carefully. Nobody, she felt sure, would object to her going down to the
gardens, but it could be embarrassing to bump into a member of the family she did not know. Because of this she
avoided the main staircase, certain there must be other ways
of getting below. Turning left instead of right, she went off
on what she only intended to be a very small journey of
exploration.

She did, in fact, get quite a way, further than she realised.
Several of the doors were ajar, opening on to what appeared
to be empty rooms, and her confidence grew as no one
disturbed her. Then suddenly to her dismay a woman,
obviously another servant, called her.

'*Mademoiselle*!' Slightly breathless, the woman caught her
up. Ross stopped nervously and turned. 'Mademoiselle Lindsay?' the newcomer asked softly, and when Ross nodded,
said, 'My lady saw you passing by and would like very much
to speak with you.'

Such gentle, soft-voiced courtesy was scarcely to be with-
stood, yet uncertainly Ross hesitated. Who was 'my lady'? In
the Near East, she had read, a man might have many

relations living in his household. Lone sisters, aunts and
elderly parents were never left simply to fend for themselves,
and a house this size could probably accommodate vast
numbers. They would hardly be noticed. Whoever wished to
speak to her must be one of these, she decided. Someone
with little to do, consumed by a little harmless curiosity?

Nodding, Ross returned the servant's tentative smile, and
went with her.

With her first glimpse of the apartment, however, realisation flooded Ross that here was no set of rooms belonging to
a poor relation. Here there was understated opulence, reflecting the grandeur she had seen downstairs. The beauty of the
rooms, the furniture, the skins and rugs on the floor, the
gold-threaded drapes, made her catch her breath. So confused was she that she might have turned and run if it had
not been for the woman who walked towards her as she
stood slightly dazed by the entrance.

The woman, too, made Ross catch her breath. She was
beautiful, was Ross's first thought. About the same height
and size as herself, she was dressed simply but smartly in a
silken caftan. Her hair was dark, coiled at the back of her
smooth head, and she was skilfully if discreetly made up.
She wasn't so very young any more, possibly in her sixties,
but her beauty was of the kind that would be ageless.

To Ross's surprise she approached with her hand out-
stretched, her manner most friendly. 'You are Mademoiselle
Lindsay?' she exclaimed. 'I saw you passing and could not
resist sending my nurse after you. I am Armel's aunt, Yvette.
You met my husband, the Caid, when you arrived. I am
sorry I was not there to welcome you.'

Ross's wide glance of swift surprise was not, she hoped,
impertinent. 'I'm sorry,' she breathed, unsteadily, 'I'm afraid
I didn't realise, *madame*. I didn't expect ... I mean, Armel,
that is,' she corrected hastily, 'Sidi ben Yussef told me you
were ill and I thought you would be in bed.'

Madame appeared to find nothing strange in Ross's confused, unfinished remarks. She smiled quite sympathetically,
as if something faintly amused her. 'Of course, my child, you
are naturally perplexed, and with just cause. Come,' she

released Ross's hand and stepped back, waving her imperiously into an elegant drawing room, 'you must take coffee
with me. A few days confined to my rooms and I am bored
to distraction.'

For several minutes she chatted gaily in French, then
changed into English which, like Armel's, was accentuated
just enough to give it an added attraction. 'Armel has explained how you were parted from your half-brother,' she
said, on a more sober note. 'It is a great pity, as he is so
much older and more travelled than you, that he didn't plan
your itinerary more carefully.'

As Ross was unaware of the exact context of Armel's ex-
planations she could only remain silent. 'You are very kind,
madame, to take a complete stranger into your home,' she
heard herself saying diffidently.

'Oh, as to that, Mademoiselle Lindsay, I can only say I
have complete faith in my nephew's judgment—and my own
eyes. He would never bring me someone who is not wholly
acceptable.'

What did she mean by that? On the face of it there was
nothing but warm politeness, yet underneath Ross sensed
subtle undertones which disconcerted. She said, unconsciously defensive, not hearing the slight tremor in her voice,
'Thank you, *madame*, but I should not have come if your
son had not sought out Sidi ben Yussef in the desert. I'm
afraid there wasn't time to make other arrangements.'

'And I'm so glad, *mademoiselle*,' the other woman smiled
warmly. 'Armel tells me you are willing to stay on a while to
help with my correspondence until I get a little stronger.
This has already made me feel much better. It also made me
very curious to meet you.' She picked up the coffee pot while
regarding Ross keenly. 'You are a pretty child. I think I shall
enjoy having you around.'

Ross felt her cheeks flush as she again murmured polite
appreciation. There was a faint bewilderment in her eyes as
she watched the nurse firmly take over the pouring of the
coffee and listened to the short ensuing argument which
Madame appeared to lose. Obviously the nurse was a privi-
leged member of the household. Somehow Madame looked

different from the usual Moroccan lady. She shared their elegance, but there the similarity ended. Ross had never known her before, yet she seemed in some inexplicable way to be familiar.

'I hope I shall be able to fulfil your requirements, *madame*,' she continued rather helplessly, when the nurse passed her refreshments and moved away. 'I'm afraid,' she confessed in a dismal rush, 'Sidi ben Yussef told me to wait in my room.'

'Do you always call him that?' Madame glanced up from her coffee idly, not obviously quelled by the thought of her nephew's possible displeasure. 'Hasn't he explained about his name, or did you not come to know him well enough?'

Ross looked quickly down at her cup, having the sudden impression that this woman, like her devious nephew, was capable of probing, if unobtrusively. 'He did once ask me to call him Armel,' she admitted cautiously.

'And you found this difficult, *ma chère*? Just as he can be a very difficult man . . .' Her deep sigh seemed to speak of past conflicts. 'Occasionally I even fail to understand him myself, but this was not quite what I meant. I think if you are to stay and work here that you should know who he really is.'

'Really is, *madame*?' Ross felt her fingers curling tightly into her palms. 'I'm afraid I don't understand,' she whispered, trying to speak normally but failing oddly.

'My nephew's real name is Guerard, child. Armel Guerard, and he is French. He is also a well-known surgeon.'

For a long moment Ross stared numbly at her clenched hands. She felt strange, quite cold inside in spite of the heat of the day. So this was what he was? And he wasn't Moroccan after all but French. His aunt must be, too, which explained a lot. Or should do, when she was capable of thinking it out! How hadn't she guessed? Hadn't she felt all along that he was different? The bleak feeling increased three-fold. Why hadn't he told her?

Her paling face must have alarmed the woman sitting opposite. 'I hope this hasn't disturbed you, child. I find it hard to believe he said nothing.'

'No,' Ross confessed, trying to hide her deep misery, 'There was no reason why he should, *madame*.' Deliberately she forced herself to ask, 'Why, if Monsieur Guerard is a famous surgeon, does he spend so much time in the desert, and under a different name?'

CHAPTER TEN

MADAME leant forward eagerly, clearly more than willing to talk of her own family, to give Ross the information she so painfully sought. 'My father, Armel's grandfather, was with one of the French regiments when Morocco was a French protectorate. My brother and I spent much time here, and it was here that I met the Caid and married him. My brother, Armel's father, married a French girl, but they were both killed in an accident when he was little more than a baby. He was a delightful baby, *mademoiselle*, and my husband and I brought him up. He went to school in France, then on to university, but all his holidays he spent with us. I believe he is still fonder of Morocco than France, although he practised there.'

She paused, as if the next bit was not going to be so easy to relate. 'He was brilliant and became extremely well known. Then he crashed his car one evening. He had been operating all day and was undoubtedly overtired, but he naturally blamed himself.'

'Why naturally, *madame*?'

'Why?' Madame sighed resignedly. 'Don't we always? There was no one else involved. He crashed into a tree, but his fingers were badly crushed and he couldn't operate any more. I think because of this he became very bitter, or maybe it was because his fiancée gave him up. Anyway, he left everything and came here to do research work. The well-being of our desert tribes has always been near to his heart. A lot of these people still refuse to see a doctor, and there are pockets of disease, as there are still in many countries. To use another name has made it easier for him to work in many areas, although he has always had the full blessing of the authorities. He doesn't, of course, receive any payment, nor does he ask for any, but already he has merited much acclaim.'

'I see,' Ross whispered, scarcely able to find the voice to speak at all. So Armel had been famous, was famous, and had had a fiancée! Somehow it was this latter that hurt more than anything else. 'I knew none of this,' she admitted slowly, 'although some of it, I suppose, I might have guessed.' It was only too easy to realise now what he had been doing out in the desert, and during all those long hours he had spent in his tent. And she had called him a brigand! 'I do know about his fingers, but he gave me no details.' She hesitated. 'I believe he was annoyed when I could see little wrong with them.' She shivered as she recalled how he had deliberately used them on her body as if to punish her for tact he in no way appreciated.

His aunt was nodding, as if what Ross said agreed with her own views. 'I have reason to believe he might go back to surgery, perhaps sooner than we had hoped.'

Ross said uncertainly, 'Perhaps you shouldn't be telling me this? I'm not sure that Armel—Monsieur Guerard—would wish you to.'

'I realise, *ma chère*,' Madame grimaced charmingly, 'but I feel I must tell someone. I'm having the greatest difficulty in keeping it to myself.' Her dark eyes, so like Armel's, snapped, and again she leant towards Ross eagerly. 'About three weeks ago I had a heart attack. Just a slight one, I admit, but it made me feel quite ill for a time. I have an excellent doctor who flies here if necessary, and, just as I began to feel better, I have this phone call from Armel's fiancée—his ex-fiancée, you understand?'

The cold in Ross turned swiftly to ice, but she was able to nod.

'It seems,' Madame continued, 'she wishes to see him again, to be, how is it you say, united. That she regrets what she did to him, the pain she caused him, very much. She is convinced that he still loves her but that he is too proud to seek her out. This is why she is coming here, why she begged me to find Armel, so that they might be together again. I felt his happiness was at stake, that my illness was an excuse provided by a benevolent fate to get him from the desert so that they might settle their differences. So immedi-

ately I sent Moulay, my only son, to fetch him, ostensibly for
my benefit, of course.'

'I see.' Ross scarcely recognised the flatness of her own
voice. So this was how it was with Armel. Well, he had
never pretended there could be anything between them but
antagonism, so she had no reason to feel so tragic. She could
see now why he had not allowed her one glimpse into his
private life. To discover he was French was not totally surprising, not after the first shock had worn off, but that he
was a famous surgeon put him miles beyond her own
humble status. How he must have laughed at her recklessly
sweeping assumptions that he was a common, low-down
thief!

As if this was not enough it seemed he had a fiancée, a girl
whom he loved. The distress Ross had suffered overnight
because of Freddy and Cynthia receded into the background
when faced with this new torment. With Freddy and Cynthia it had been nothing she had not known before in vary-
ing degrees, but this was something entirely outside any
previous experience, a vicious kind of torture. She had been
half resigned to remaining here for at least a while, not
having been able to resist the idea of helping Armel. Unconsciously, perhaps, she had hoped to see the friction between them dissolving when he learnt how efficient she
could be? Had there also been, she wondered heavily, rosy,
improbable dreams of the future? Of Armel and herself in
the desert, of directing him away from dishonest activities to
something useful? How utterly crazy she had been to have
ever visualised the two of them finding a lasting happiness
together beneath the lonely desert skies!

'Will his fiancée be long in coming?' she asked slowly,
aware vaguely that Madame awaited her comment.

'No!' Madame appeared exhausted but eminently satisfied
with herself. 'She is an American, so you will understand
that travel is no problem, especially as she is wealthy! She
will arrive any time, but then we are prepared. Of course
. . .' momentarily a frown stilled her tinkling laughter, 'I
must ask you not to say anything of this to Armel. I'm afraid
I have been rather indiscreet, but as a personal secretary you

must be used to such confidences, and the keeping of them, I
feel sure.'

'Yes, *madame*.'

'I have only his happiness at heart!' Madame smiled bril-
liantly, a smile that faded somewhat swiftly as the door
opened without warning and Armel strode in.

'Good morning, Yvette,' he said dryly, 'I hope your health
continues to improve. I still can't think why you thought me
necessary!' His cryptic glance went straight to Ross and it
was easy to see he was extremely displeased about something.
'I trust also that Mademoiselle Lindsay has been keeping you
sufficiently entertained?' Startling them both, he swung
almost savagely to Ross. 'Did I not tell you to stay in your
room?'

'I . . .'

'The girl,' Madame intervened quickly, 'was simply on her
way to the gardens, Armel, when I happened to see her pass.
I merely called her in for coffee. Will you not have some?'

Coffee not being the wisest choice at that particular moment, he refused. 'No!'

How curt he could be when he chose! Ross glanced at him
trying, in a confused fashion, to recall his softer moods but
there was nothing in his face this morning to invite pro-
longed inspection, only everything to deter it. His anger, at
her apparent disregard for his orders, appeared to be sur-
facing and she could not sustain the glacial narrowness of his
eyes.

Madame, possibly because of her high station in life,
proved quicker witted in such situations. Milder remarks,
she obviously sensed, would be lost on her nephew right
now. She must provide something more effective, one which
might remove the onus from herself.

'I am surprised to learn, *chéri*, that you omitted to inform
Mademoiselle Lindsay of your true identity? That you are
French.'

Armel's fingers, curling around Ross's wrist in the act of
yanking her to her feet, tightened perceptibly and the ensuing jerk landed her within inches of his imperiously
straight nose. 'Since when was it any of her—of your busi-

ness, *mademoiselle*!' His words swung harshly from his
aunt to herself, almost as if it were she who had reproached
him.

Ross heard herself replying tautly, 'I am not complaining,
monsieur. It is natural enough that your aunt should be
surprised. After all, it would have been easy enough to have
told me.'

'And because I didn't choose to, you behave like a sulky
child, even to the droop of your provoking lips. Your wilful-
ness has never been concealed from me. It makes me regret I
didn't deal with you, out there in the desert, as I often felt
tempted to!'

'Please!' Ross whispered urgently, her throat strangled,
'your aunt, *monsieur*!' She was aware that Madame listened
to Armel with a kind of bewildered sharpness in her eyes, as
if something lay just beyond her comprehension, some knowledge, almost within reach, that annoyed her by its evasive-
ness. Ross added, as Armel neither moved or appeared about
to shut up, 'I really don't think Madame is well enough to be
upset by such a senseless conversation! I disrupted, if unintentionally, your routine in the desert and you were naturally annoyed, but there was no indiscretion that need worry
your aunt.'

Two minutes later Ross was again standing in her own
room, having been torn from Madame's apartments and
along the corridor before she quite realised what was happening. Here Armel flung her arm away, as if such contact
burnt him, leaving her to stare at him unhappily as he strode
to the window and stood staring out. It wouldn't be the
mountains he contemplated so grimly, but her growing
number of sins. She supposed it might be tactful to apologise
for disobeying his orders, but somehow could not. This
morning, dressed as he was in a light shirt and dark slacks
which moulded his long, powerful legs, his head bare, his
hair brushed back thickly, he did look French. This, along
with other things she had just learnt, made him seem too
much of a stranger to make such overtures possible.

But surely he had no right to regard her as if she had
committed a crime of unheard-of enormity! Hadn't he been

guilty of far worse things himself? Hurt began to push aside her indignation. Yet the pain she felt now would be nothing she knew to that which would develop when she had time to fully digest all Madame had told her about his fiancée! She had promised not to mention it, a promise that hadn't really been necessary, as Armel's personal life could have nothing to do with her. Even his career, as he had so recently and decisively pointed out, was none of her business!

Then, as his silence unnerved her more than she liked, she faltered to his broad back, 'I'm sorry you feel so strongly about what I did, that I left my room when you told me not to, but your aunt was nice to me and I'm sure she didn't betray any confidences deliberately. Apparently she had no idea you hadn't mentioned your true nationality. It would, as I have already pointed out, have been extremely easy.'

'Quite,' he agreed hardly, swinging around to face her, 'but you scarcely invited such confidences, did you! You were so sure I was every type of criminal rolled into one. I don't think I exaggerate to say you looked at me often as if you went in fear, even of your life?'

'No,' she cried. 'Well, maybe,' she confessed reluctantly, her eyes falling guiltily from his.

'Maybe!' He was by her side again, his hold hurting. 'There was no doubt about it, fair Rosalind! I meant to make you pay dearly for such undisguised condemnation. Shall we say it became a challenge I couldn't resist? In that you can justifiably relegate me to the ranks of a fool! That I did not take into consideration the enticement of a slim white body, eyes and lips which lured and bewitched, even as they denied, *mademoiselle*, the final taking!'

'I did nothing to encourage such—such advances,' Ross stammered, unable to meet the flare of something unrecognisable in his eyes, her heart throbbing so she knew he must feel it. 'Shouldn't you,' she went on desperately, 'be glad you did nothing—er—indiscreet? Nothing which could sully your reputation.'

'As a member of my profession, you mean?' His head went back and he laughed unkindly. '*Mon dieu*! And you are not even my patient! So you really think I was bound by such ethics? I left my profession formally, *mademoiselle*, when I was no longer able to use these!' He flung up his hand and her dazed glance rested on his two scarred fingers.

'They look almost perfect now, *monsieur*. I can't think they can be a handicap any longer.'

His mouth thinned as he nodded, but it was not as if her words appeared to give much comfort. Impatiently he retorted, 'This I realise. I seem to have regained complete flexibility and am considering returning to France. After I have satisfactorily concluded my work here.'

'Then you should no longer feel bitter! Unless...' her voice trailed off. Almost she had betrayed her knowledge of his fiancée. Very nearly she had assured him that all his dreams were on the verge of coming true, not just one of them. That the past was about to compensate him fully for what it had done to him. Her hands were tied, hadn't she promised? Besides, why subject herself to the pain of witnessing his joyful anticipation of another woman?

Armel Guerard waited, still impatient. 'Second thoughts, *chérie*?' he queried sauvely as she refused to finish her sentence.

'Some things,' she muttered, 'are better left unsaid. Or perhaps I should say some things are best found out for ourselves.'

'And what,' he sneered sarcastically, 'am I supposed to conclude from that?'

'Nothing that is going to make you unhappy, *monsieur*,' she cried, her blue eyes almost blurred with her own despair. 'Anyway, I wish you every success, in everything,' she added stiffly, as if they were already wishing each other goodbye.

A moment's enigmatic pause. 'Success,' he rejoined dryly, 'is very rarely all that it seems. I imagined I was relatively successful with women once. Until I met you.'

Had his voice softened? Had his eyes, his sensuous mouth taken on a gentle irony, as if he sought some assurance only she could give? If only she could tell him that in a very short time all his confidence in that direction would be restored. His fiancée should be with him, probably within hours. All Ross could hope for with reasonable expectation was that she might be spared the agony of seeing them meet.

'You don't speak!' He studied her, and if she had been unsure of the warmth there was no mistaking his coldness. 'Occasionally,' he added, 'I suspect it pleases you to appear somewhat disturbed, so that I must seek every answer myself. Come here, you little deceiver!'

Before Ross could move his arms went out to draw her to him, slipping around her slender back so forcibly as to make her realise it would be useless to fight him. But she didn't want to—it was a fault in her that she never wanted to! Her eyes widened, then closed, her whole body responding to the hardness of his touch. She turned up her mouth, uninvited, as he lowered his, feeling the same urgent desire as her body moulded itself against his hard frame.

His hand came up, spreading and tugging through her tumbled hair, and she half lay against him, her balance gone. His mouth trailed over the soft skin of her cheek to the bare curve of her neck, seeking out each sensitive hollow as he bent her back over his arm. There were waves of white shooting stars breaking into shattering fragments about her head, and her lips parted as at last his returned to plunder them unmercifully. His voice was low, murmuring between kisses and she heard herself whisper his name as she answered him. Then, suddenly shocked by the recklessness of her own behaviour, she was pushing him away, denying that there could ever be anything between them.

She had not hoped he would let her go easily, but he did. 'I don't know why you feel you must go on punishing me,' she whispered, her face intensely white with emotion. 'You could be sorry.'

'That sounds very like a threat—or a warning?'

'No.' She must be careful! Hadn't Madame warned her not to say anything?

Armel stood back, his eyes glinting coolly. 'Well, I am about to issue both! An order, if you like, and I have no wish to be disobeyed! I will send a girl to take you down to the gardens. Afterwards you will be served with a light lunch in your room. This evening you will join the family for dinner, to which I will personally escort you. My aunt will be there, for a little while. I am telling you this as you appear to derive more comfort from her presence than mine.'

Again, as he paused derisively, Ross wondered drearily how he could so quickly detach himself from the emotional scenes they so frequently shared. It pointed to only one thing, and she didn't care to think about it. Tears stung her eyes, the desolate tears which of late had been coming too frequently. He was in no way involved, not as she was!

He continued, 'As it seems you are particularly resilient you can begin working tomorrow on those letters which she feels can be put off no longer. But that is all! In a few days' time you could probably do a certain amount for me. We shall see.'

We shall see! Ross's chin lifted angrily. It was his arrogant way of taking supreme command of the situation! Did she have no say in the matter? 'You may find in the next few days, *monsieur*, you don't need me at all!' There was so much emphasis in her voice as to indicate unmistakably that there was at least one thing he wasn't aware of. That he had a shock of some sort coming.

His mouth moved to a guarded line of suspicion, his eyes piercing on the surge of guilty, defiant colour in her face. 'What exactly has Yvette been up to now?' he snapped instantly. 'Just what has she been saying?'

Her nerve cowardly dispersing, Ross shivered unhappily. 'Why, nothing,' she faltered, wishing desperately for even a little of Armel's icy control. Before it her attack lay weakly shattered. 'What would she tell me—a stranger!'

'What indeed!' He was by no means pacified. 'After over thirty years in her position one might imagine she must have learnt all about discretion, but there are still times when she fails to stop and think before she speaks.'

'I'm sure you have no reason to judge her so unkindly,' Ross exclaimed, regretting again that she could not tell him all his aunt was doing for him. The happiness which was soon to be his. Hadn't she said too much already?

He ignored this, the set of his mouth no kinder as his eyes remained fixed on her revealing face. 'So I am not to be enlightened? Sometimes I think you make a much better enemy, *ma chère*, than a friend!' He slaughtered her with another withering look, then swung on his heel.

The girl came, though, as he had promised, and showed her how to find her way to the gardens. Ross, who was beginning to feel very curious about this Moroccan household, would have liked to explore herself, but keeping in mind her first disaster of an hour ago, she obediently followed her guide. She was aware there might be several members of the family she had yet to meet, but realised that routine here might be very different from the English one she was used to. There would be, in a house like this, a great deal of formality. People did not just wander in and out. She had no idea how it would be in many of the smaller dwellings of the *kasbah*, but here she had already noticed several guards who, she suspected, were armed. Armel had mentioned that the Caid was a man of some importance. He had also told her that the Caid usually entertained foreign visitors himself in his country home, his wife only appearing on family occasions. In Ross's opinion this seemed to amount to something approaching the old feudalism, and she regretted the wistful thought that it might be wonderfully nice to be a woman and so protected against any possible rigours of the outside world. It was perhaps some of this apparently feudal system that had rubbed off on Armel and helped to make him what he was. If he had grown up here it must have done.

The gardens were, to Ross's surprise, beautiful, if not gardens in the true English sense of the word. They were more in the nature of deep green patios, cool and shady under densely planted trees. Many of the trees were fig and peach, but some were orange, and heavily laden with large, still green fruit. There were clumps of geraniums and sweet-smelling roses and in the middle of a wide paved area a fountain played, cascading its cool sprays of water into a shimmering pool at its feet. After the heat and dust of the desert the sight of such cool, cultivated greenness seemed too great a contrast to be instantly believable and for several minutes Ross found she could only stand and stare.

The air from the mountains was warmly seductive and

reality faded. There came in its place a curiously free impression, a whisper of the harem of long ago. Of veiled and shrouded beauties, of nymphs, a houri of alluring loveliness with jewel-studded chains at her ankles and wrists, dancing voluptuously before her lord and master to the tinkling accompaniment of the two-stringed mandolin. All her desires, her racing pulse would be in tune with the throbbing heartbeats of the dark-eyed, watching man.

It took the galloping hooves of a squad of the Caid's horsemen, the derisive scream of a low-flying jet to break through her spellbound thoughts, making her conscious that she lived in a vastly different century, one far removed from that of her foolish imagination. But in her dreams she had seen herself as a dancer, Armel in the sheik's dark, hooded face . . .

Despondent, and curiously exhausted by an intensity of such unguarded emotion, she sank down on one of the flat stones by the fountain, her head drooping, her slim white fingers trailing the water. What was Armel doing at this moment? she wondered, unable to keep him long from her thoughts. Was he already making arrangements for his return to France, where his aunt had hinted he had much property to look after as well as his career? She must spend time thinking about her own future—what she would do when she left here? Thoughts of England were engulfed in loneliness and, like a coward, she jumped again to her feet, searching for some new diversion, so that she might banish even the mental picture of it from her mind.

That evening Ross dined with the Caid and his family. With Armel by her side she met more aunts and cousins than she ever suspected existed. Possibly because she had so few relatives herself she found herself considering them eagerly, trying to attach small histories to each one of them as, apparently, most of them lived more or less permanently at the *kasbah*. If they were a little reticent at first, they were soon chatting to Ross pleasantly, obviously taking an instant liking to the young English girl whom Armel appeared to watch over very closely. Moulay was there. He had, Ross learnt, three sisters, all married, who lived elsewhere. He

was very circumspect, so very proper that Ross was inclined
to forget the languishing glances he had cast over her in the
desert, his smiles, if discreet, which had caused Armel to
round on her with such fury. Now Moulay was merely
pleasantly friendly. Only his eyes showed a certain amount of
interest.

The Caid greeted her charmingly, asking her a little about
her homeland, which, as he moved in the highest diplomatic
circles, she wasn't surprised to find he knew quite well.
After a few such remarks he said reminiscently, 'I'm afraid
the only Lindsay I ever knew was a foreign correspondent
who was killed, not on the assignment he had just covered,
but when his plane crashed in the desert. You remember it,
Armel, about ten years ago?'

As Armel thought for a moment, then nodded vaguely,
Ross said quietly, 'That was my father. It was one of the
reasons why I agreed to come here.'

While the Caid murmured his genuine surprise and regret, Ross became aware of Armel's tight-lipped expression.
She doubted if it was sympathy for something that had happened so long ago. She had never intended to mention her
father, or how he had died, but in view of what the Caid
knew it would have been silly to have said nothing. He
might easily have found out.

It was not until the Caid moved away that Armel murmured sardonically in her ear, 'So I continue to learn, girl? I
wonder what will be next!'

'Nothing that could compare with all I have learnt about
you, monsieur,' she assured him, glad in every part of her
when his aunt came up and took her away to talk to the
other women. Yet she didn't escape so easily. She was conscious of his grim gaze following her the entire evening.

Ross was not there the next day when the plane carrying
Armel's ex-fiancée arrived from Tangier. The maid brought
the news with her lunch which she was having in her room
after spending a pleasant hour with Armel's aunt. Ross had
been worried that her French might not be good enough, in
spite of the care Armel had taken, but she had found it
sufficed. Madame had been pleased with her. By mutual, if

unspoken, agreement Armel had not been mentioned. Now
this news of his friend's arrival brought pain surging afresh.
Her self-protective instincts curiously sensitive, she decided
to stay in her room, but as the afternoon wore on this became
clearly impossible. Eventually, unable to bear her own wretch-
edness any longer, she crept like a shadow down to the
garden.

Unfortunately she met Moulay on one of the long, light
corridors which seemed never-ending. As he saw her approaching his good-natured face broke into a warm smile
and he bowed slightly from the waist, asking her where she
was off to in his excellent French. They were all so kind,
Ross thought distractedly, always remembering she spoke no
Arabic.

'Down to the patio for an hour as I've nothing else to do,'
she answered quickly. Then, feeling rather ashamed of such
abruptness, 'Yesterday I found your gardens very pleasant.'

'Yes.' Moulay did not appear to be considering the splend-
ours outside. 'I should like to accompany you,' he said earn-
estly, 'especially as my dear cousin has someone else to take
his attention this afternoon! It seems sad that I must go
immediately to Marrakesh on urgent business. I should have
gone days ago but, as you know, I was seeking Armel. And
because, for some mysterious reason, my efforts seem to have
been wasted, my good father is more than usually impatient.'

Ross thought she understood. Moulay's mother had told
neither her son or husband her real reason for wanting
Armel's return. No doubt they would soon learn! 'Madame
obviously has confidence in him when she is ill,' she observed
tactfully.

Moulay nodded, having a genuine appreciation of his
cousin's expertise. 'He saved my mother's life a few years
ago. She has now repaid him by asking a very dear friend of
his to visit. A charming American, *mademoiselle*.'

'And one whom he loves!'

'My mother believes so.'

'And you . . .?' Why was she punishing herself so, poun-
cing so hungrily, and with a complete lack of dignity, on

Moulay's slight hesitation? 'I expect you think so too?' she mumbled hurriedly, trying to conceal such an indecent searching after crumbs.

His dark eyes narrowed, suddenly too keen, reminding her too uncomfortably of Armel. 'Would it matter to you whether he loves this woman or not?'

'No—of course not!' How easily she lied! Unnatural colour flared in her cheeks. 'Monsieur Guerard is returning to France. He will wish for the kind of wife who will fit into his world. He rescued me in the desert, he was kind to me. How could I not wish him every happiness?'

'But you, Mademoiselle Rosalind, you would fit into his world too!' Moulay laughed softly down at her. 'You are young, beautiful and learn easily. You have also a certain delicate air of breeding, if that does not sound old-fashioned. If we are to look for faults then perhaps you are a little like myself, too impulsive. How long has Armel lectured me on this failing! I have a faint suspicion he sees the same thing in you, and believes you should be given time to correct it.'

Ross blinked on a drawn breath, staring at Moulay, attempting to fathom what he was trying to say—to tell her? But before she could ask for a clearer explanation he was gone. 'I'll see you when I return, *ma chère*!' he laughed, as if there was no reason at all why either of them should be miserable.

She continued her way to the terraces, her heart refusing to be comforted by his devious optimism. Yet Moulay had provided a little diversion and she was grateful, even if she still failed to understand what he meant. He had gone to a famous English school, and could be, when he felt inclined, a curious mixture of East and West. Or maybe the confusion lay only in herself? She couldn't, however, see how her impulsiveness could affect Armel, even if he was astute enough to realise she was prone to it!

Down in the courtyards she sought out the one where the fountain played, but the happily splashing water, misted to gold in the sparkling sunlight, was so discordant with her present mood that she couldn't stay. Instead she wandered until she found another spot, this one darkly shaded by overhanging branches, quite a way from the main residence. It had obviously not been used for a long time. There were probably snakes and all sorts of things waiting to attack her as she invaded their privacy, but she could not seem to care. It looked as good a place as any other to hide her heartache from the outside world.

Although she did not intend to weep, such lengthy contemplation of Armel and his woman friend eventually brought tears. Against the low stone parapet, beside which lovers must no doubt once have wandered, she sobbed quietly, until at last, exhausted by the cold despair inside her, her fair head drooped to the warm stone and she slept.

A long time later she dreamt she was running towards Armel, but just as his arms reached out to catch her, she woke up, for a dazed moment having no idea where she was. It was almost dark and the shadows were long, although she was not cold. The quivering of her body could only be from reaction, as Armel was nowhere to be seen.

Numbly she raised her hand to brush the tangled hair from her face. She must look a mess, with bits of dirt and leaves clinging to her hot skin. If she went straight to her room it was unlikely she would be seen, then, after she had washed, she would go immediately to bed. Her aching head would provide a truthful excuse to miss dinner, to avoid meeting the girl who by this time must surely, once again, be Armel's fiancée.

In her room Ross did not switch on the light right away. Her eyes felt too sore and strained to bear it and aimlessly she wandered to the window, wondering vaguely where she might best find some aspirin. Probably she should ring for the maid?

Seconds later she nearly jumped out of her skin when the door opened and someone spoke her name. Of what use was the swift prayer that it might be her maid? Even before he spoke she had known it was Armel.

'Rosalind!' It came like a pistol shot, laced with impatience. 'What on earth are you doing standing here in the

dark? Or should I say, where have you been? I came to take
you to dinner and couldn't find you. I've been distracted,
girl!'

Still she didn't turn—she could not. Not on any account
must he see her face. 'I'm sorry,' she managed, her voice
husky from tears. 'I went for a walk as I'd a headache. I
don't want any dinner. I'm not hungry. If you would just
go!'

Silence!

'Your fiancée,' she choked, bent on self-punishment, 'will
be waiting.'

Now he really did move. He was across the room in two
strides, his hands on her shaking shoulders, pulling her
around to him. If he was shocked by her ravaged face, in the
light from the doorway, he didn't say so, but his hands
tightened perceptibly and his breathing changed.

'What do you know about my—er—fiancée?' he snapped,
at last.

'Nothing . . .'

'So that was what Yvette was talking about!' he exclaimed
curtly, ignoring her denial.

'No, Armel!' Ross's voice broke with the force of her
apprehension. 'Well, yes,' she confessed helplessly, before the
relentless glitter in his eyes, 'she did say something, but it
can't matter now, not when you have what you want.'

'I haven't—yet.'

That went over Ross's head. 'She knew how much you
loved her.'

'Women!' It was an exasperated snort, but his anger
seemed miraculously to be fading. He even smiled, which,
Ross decided, was brutally unkind, as it must be at her own
dishevelled appearance. 'I don't have any fiancée,' he went
on to inform her suavely, 'although I hope to. Would you
feel any better, I wonder, if I told you that the particular
lady you are thinking of has been and gone?'

'You mean . .'

'Come, Rosalind!' Suddenly he was adamant. 'The atmosphere here is not quite the way I like it. We will grab some

transport and I'll show you the mountains in the moonlight. It has always been my intention to do so. Events have merely precipitated this a little. We'll raid the kitchens when we return—I'll almost guarantee you have an appetite then!'

The mountains of the Middle Atlas are magnificent at any time, but by moonlight they reminded Ross of great pagan gods, stalking the bare, stony landscape, searching hungrily if still majestically for a greener land on which to set their jagged peaks.

Armel had said little and Ross had been too dazed to say anything at all as he had literally taken her prisoner and, under his absolute control, brought her out here. The isolation was so complete, their surroundings so stark, they might have been anywhere between heaven and earth, lost forever in measureless wastes of space and—tranquillity. How deceptive appearances could be, Ross thought bleakly, as he parked the vehicle on the extreme crest of a rocky plateau with nothing, so far as she could see, below or beyond.

'*Monsieur*,' her voice suddenly cracked as she stared around her nervously, 'are you sure this is safe?'

'No.' He said nothing to reassure her as he turned slowly, reaching for her. 'But you might be safer out there, *mademoiselle*, than you could be in my arms!'

Ross's breath really did fail her now. What had she done, allowing herself to be dragged up here, by a man who must only regard her as an object of amusement? Where was her good sense, her pride? Did her heart have to throb so with his breath on her cheek, his arms closing tightly around her trembling body?

'Armel!' She had to speak, but apparently he was of the opinion they had wasted too much time already. Taking no notice of her anguished plea, he thrust back her head, his fingers determined under her chin.

'You are going to tell me this instant what all these tears are about? This aura of unhappiness that is quite unmistakable!'

For Ross the time for subterfuge had passed. There was nothing she could do but answer, not with his intent, merciless gaze fixed so unwaveringly on her. 'It was because of your visitor, the girl you love,' she whispered, through frozen lips.

He had the nerve to smile! With abject despair she watched it spread with a trace of complacency across his face. 'It pleases you to laugh!' she cried, on the verge of anger.

His mirth, if that was what it had been, faded. 'Oh, Rosalind,' he said softly as he lowered his head, 'the small rose with the thorns that I found in my desert!' His mouth found hers, as it had done so many times before, and we was gentle, yet he was not gentle at all. He carried her with him ruthlessly through dizzying heights of sensation, until she could only cling to him, unable to disguise any longer the desire which threatened to consume her. His arms were hard and she could feel the mounting strength of his passion until, at last, with a frustrated groan, he released her and she turned her burning lips against his throat.

He said, his face pale, his voice curiously sober, 'Do you think I could kiss you like that if I loved another woman? Didn't you realise it was you I cared about? You whom I love?'

Ross couldn't believe it, not to begin with. 'But this girl?' she raised her head and tried to search his dark face. 'The one you were engaged to.'

'Dearest,' there was a slight smile again as he drew her back to him, 'I can see you won't rest until I explain about her. It was three years ago, we were both in our early thirties, and it was a sort of mutual agreement. She was looking for an ambitious, well-known husband—she didn't need wealth as she has more than enough of her own. Besides, I have a certain amount myself and I was also thinking of a wife. I imagined it might lend a certain dignity to my career, and as I had never been in love I was of the firm conviction, by this time, that it simply did not exist. I was still of this belief until I met you, *chérie*!'

'But why did you break your engagement?' Ross asked faintly.

'I didn't,' he confessed briefly. 'It was she, and I must admit that for a long while it made me feel bitter. When my hand was damaged and it seemed I would never be able to operate again she found I was no longer attractive. She even said my injuries were repulsive, although I expect this was more of an excuse.'

'Then why did she return today?'

'I'm afraid my well-meaning aunt told her I was likely to resume my work in Paris, and Rona had found no one to take my place. This afternoon, my darling, it was my un-fortunate task to persuade her that she really didn't want me at all, that she would be much wiser to concentrate on the obviously adoring admirer who brought her here in his plane.'

Wide-eyed, Ross gazed at him tremulously. 'You didn't seem to so much as like me. You thought me too impulsive!'

'Yes . . .' He covered her face with soft kisses. 'But what else was I to think, you little wretch! You had followed your half-brother so blindly into an impossible situation, and did the most foolish things. But it was my own emotions I understood least, something I in no way appreciated! I felt I had to be harsh, otherwise I might easily become demented! I can't truthfully say I fell in love the first moment I saw you,' he teased wryly. 'It took me several hours to com-prehend why a man of my wide experience should have been so shocked by that first moving little act of yours in the nomad's tent. Why I was so struck by a pair of dazzling blue eyes. For what you made me feel, I wanted to both love and punish you at the same time. When you ran off with Salem it was bad enough, but when Moulay turned up I think I went occasionally quite mad with jealousy, *mignonne*. I vowed I'd carry you off and force you to marry me there and then, but of course I had to remember how young you were, that you probably didn't know your own mind. Then, when we returned here and I spoke with your relatives and realised how they thought of you, how they had treated you, I was even more convinced you must be given a chance to know something more of life. Why,' he tilted her chin to look closely at her again, 'I wasn't even sure that you loved me.'

'But I did, all along!' Ross whispered fervently. 'At least,' she amended to his slightly raised eyebrows, 'I think I realised the first time you kissed me. I wanted to be near you always, yet I grew so frightened of my emotions I dared not stay. Like you, Armel, I had never been in love before. This was why I tried to escape with Salem. And I was jealous myself,' she admitted, shamefaced, 'even about the clothes you gave me to wear. I couldn't prevent myself wondering if they belonged to another woman.'

His white teeth glinted with a teasing amusement. 'They did, my darling—my aunt. Each time I set out on my research she always presented me with huge bundles of clothing to distribute among the poorer people who perhaps never got near a town to buy such things.'

'Oh, I see.' Ross felt her face flush with remorse at her former suspicions. 'I'm sorry, Armel . . .'

'Forget it, *ma chère*,' he commanded. 'I want you to forget a lot of things for the time being, including your family. One day we will go together and visit them, but not yet. Next year, perhaps.'

'I don't think they really mean to be unkind,' Ross excused them hastily. 'But,' her thoughts swung erratically, 'I haven't grown much older in the past few days?'

'No,' his firm mouth quirked, 'but my patience has. In fact it has quite given out! I have allowed myself to be convinced that, more than any outside experience, you need me. Your tears, this evening, *chérie*, drove me almost to distraction, and if you love me at least half as much as I love you, it will suffice. So, Mademoiselle Lindsay, if you can forgive all the cruel things I said to you in the desert, we will be married just as soon as it can be arranged.'

Bemused beyond words, Ross could only nod. 'I love you,' she managed at last, her eyes, very softly, seeking his.

She heard his breathing deepen, felt his mouth go tender with delight. 'Enough to perhaps live another year in the desert?' he asked.

'I don't mind where we go, as long as I am with you,' she whispered.

'Together,' he murmured thickly, finding her lips, and not

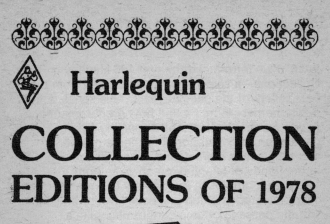

In 1976 we introduced the first 100 Harlequin Collections—a selection of titles chosen from our best sellers of the past 20 years. This series, a trip down memory lane, proved how great romantic fiction can be timeless and appealing from generation to generation. The theme of love and romance is eternal, and, when placed in the hands of talented, creative, authors whose true gift lies in their ability to write from the heart, the stories reach a special level of brilliance that the passage of time cannot dim. Like a treasured heirloom, an antique of superb craftsmanship, a beautiful gift from someone loved—these stories too, have a special significance that transcends the ordinary. **$1.25 each novel**

Here are your 1978
Harlequin Collection Editions...

Original Harlequin Romance numbers in brackets

ORDER FORM
Harlequin Reader Service

In U.S.A.
MPO Box 707
Niagara Falls, N.Y. 14302

In Canada
649 Ontario St.,
Stratford, Ontario, N5A 6W2

Please send me the following Harlequin Collection novels. I am enclosing my check or money order for $1.25 for each novel ordered, plus 25¢ to cover postage and handling.

☐ 102	☐ 115	☐ 128	☐ 140
☐ 103	☐ 116	☐ 129	☐ 141
☐ 104	☐ 117	☐ 130	☐ 142
☐ 105	☐ 118	☐ 131	☐ 143
☐ 106	☐ 119	☐ 132	☐ 144
☐ 107	☐ 120	☐ 133	☐ 145
☐ 108	☐ 121	☐ 134	☐ 146
☐ 109	☐ 122	☐ 135	☐ 147
☐ 110	☐ 123	☐ 136	☐ 148
☐ 111	☐ 124	☐ 137	☐ 149
☐ 112	☐ 125	☐ 138	☐ 150
☐ 113	☐ 126	☐ 139	☐ 151
☐ 114	☐ 127		

Number of novels checked @
$1.25 each = $ _____

N.Y. and N.J. residents add
appropriate sales tax $ _____

Postage and handling $ _____.25

TOTAL $ _____

NAME _____
(Please Print)
ADDRESS _____

CITY _____

STATE/PROV. _____

ZIP/POSTAL CODE _____

ROM 2211

A

Offer expires December 31, 1978

And there's still *more* love in

Do you have a favorite
Harlequin author?
Then here is an
opportunity you must
not miss!